A Christmas Cannoli Kiss

By

Anne Armistead

The Christmas Cookies Series

This is a work of fiction. Names, characters, places, and incidents are either the product of the author's imagination or are used fictitiously, and any resemblance to actual persons living or dead, business establishments, events, or locales, is entirely coincidental.

A Christmas Cannoli Kiss

COPYRIGHT © 2021 by Anne Armistead

All rights reserved. No part of this book may be used or reproduced in any manner whatsoever without written permission of the author or The Wild Rose Press, Inc. except in the case of brief quotations embodied in critical articles or reviews.

Contact Information: info@thewildrosepress.com

Cover Art by *Jennifer Greeff*

The Wild Rose Press, Inc.
PO Box 708
Adams Basin, NY 14410-0708
Visit us at www.thewildrosepress.com

Publishing History
First Edition, 2021
Trade Paperback ISBN 978-1-5092-4120-0
Digital ISBN 978-1-5092-4121-7

The Christmas Cookies Series
Published in the United States of America

Returning to her hometown of Pittsburgh for a girlfriend's New Year's Eve wedding inspires Isabella to move back permanently. To her surprise, she runs into her first love, Nate, fifteen years after his unexplained departure ended their teen summer romance.

Their reunion tastes as delectable as eating dessert first—until Isabella learns Nate is back to close the real estate deal between his parking lot conglomerate client and the Fontana's, the elderly couple whose beloved neighborhood bakery sits on the ideal spot for a parking deck.

Nate needs this deal to launch his career into high gear by proving his worth to his boss—his emotionally distant mother.

Isabella empathizes with the Fontana's, whom she loves like adopted grandparents. They need the sale to provide for their retirement. However, the thought of the bakery being bulldozed is breaking everyone's heart—except Nate's.

Always dreaming of owning her own café, Isabella decides to mix a different ingredient into the negotiation's 'dough.' She'll purchase the bakery and perfect the production of her mother's legendary Christmas cannoli cookies to market as its signature brand.

Isabella's cookies start to crumble, though, when she struggles to decipher her mother's handwritten recipe that's been passed down for generations and also acquire enough money to counter Nate's offer.

Concocting a way to compete against Nate puts their romance on the back burner. Can Isabella end up having her bakery—and Nate, too?

Praise for Anne Armistead

Winner of 2020 Georgia Independent Author of the Year Award, historical fiction.

Dedication

Merry Christmas, Linda Forte-Spearing.
Thanks for believing in this story every step of the way!

Chapter One

"Ladies and gentlemen, welcome to Pittsburgh. The local time is four thirteen p.m., and the temperature is a chilly thirty-four degrees with light snow. Thank you for flying with us."

Isabella's heart knocked against her chest, thumping in time with the tires as the plane taxied to the gate. She stashed her purchase of the latest thriller from the Miami airport bookstore into her handbag before craning her neck to peer out the window. At the sight of snow, little-girl excitement chased through her. A white Christmas to welcome her return after living in balmy Florida could not be more perfect.

The plane's sudden lurch to a stop jostled Isabella.

The same flight attendant's voice came across the speakers. "Ladies and gentlemen, please remain seated with your seat belts fastened while we wait for a gate. We apologize for the delay."

The older lady seated at the window seat awakened and stretched her body long.

Isabella preferred napping seat partners like hers, snores and all. She dreaded when initial chitchat with a stranger droned on and on, keeping her from reading.

Mobile phones came to life. Voices rose through the cabin in one-way conversations.

Isabella moved hers off airplane mode and scrolled through the group text she started with her close friends that morning.

They'd filled the thread with celebratory welcome home messages containing clapping hands, party hats, and thumbs-up emojis, each text bursting with confetti, balloons, or other fun effects.

Isabella hoped their excited responses meant they'd forgiven her abrupt departure after she accepted her company's transfer to Miami two years ago. She hadn't meant to worry those she held dear. Their reactions about her relocation had been upsetting.

"It's too soon after losing your parents to make a major life decision."

"You shouldn't live alone, away from those who grieve the loss of Dottie and Rico with you."

"The neighborhood won't be the same without the Lorenzo family."

None understood how the most shattering experience of her life so deeply affected her. Too many memories resided in every corner of Pittsburgh, especially her Little Italy neighborhood of Bloomfield and the intersection where the fatal car accident happened. She needed emotional space. The job in Miami provided it.

The time away helped. She gained perspective about loss and life. Two things resonated most true. One: grief found you, no matter where you lived. Two: life was too short not to pursue your dream, whatever it might be.

What better time than now to chase hers? No entanglements claimed her, not even a pet. Frugal living and a small inheritance meant she could afford a short employment sabbatical from being a brand manager while she explored a career change—a life change, really.

Isabella tossed the pouch into her bag and shifted in her seat, wondering if the plane would ever reach the gate. She gazed at that couple once again. They were engaged in a long kiss, their passion for each other pulsating through the cabin toward her.

I want that in a relationship—zing—not settling for any man in order to sport a ring on my left hand.

Attending Jen's wedding without a plus-one did not faze her. However, she did quake with fear over her agreement to bake Dottie's legendary cannoli cookies for the reception's cookie table, a Pittsburgh wedding tradition.

She once again checked inside her handbag for The Recipe to assure herself she hadn't lost it. It dated back to Isabella's maternal great-great-grandmother, Isabella de Rosa, whose first name she shared. The family matriarch recorded the cookie recipe in her spidery cursive for her daughter Francesca to bring to America. It made its way to Mom and now her.

Isabella's stomach swirled at the thought of the baking task ahead. Her friends joked she couldn't turn out edible cookies from store-bought dough. Why did she believe she could produce Mom's famous cannoli ones? Not even Angie Fontana's tasted as fabulous.

Thinking about Angie calmed Isabella's insides. Purchasing Angie's cannoli cookies from Fontana's Corner Bakery would be her backup if hers ended in disaster.

She couldn't wait to see the Fontanas again. Sal and Angie were the grandparents she'd never known. In their eighties, they remained dynamos, rising at dawn six days a week to bake their delicious breads, pastries, and cookies. When she told them of her move back, she knew from their joy her decision was the right one.

The pilot guided the plane into its assigned bay.

Passengers sprang into action before the forward motion ceased.

Isabella caught their sense of urgency to disembark. She unfastened her seat belt, sidestepped into the aisle, and donned her winter puffer coat. Its weight felt like an anchor after two years of wearing light clothing.

She moved the clothes shopping trip to the top of her long to-do list. In her anticipation of visits home, she'd kept the coat, the fur lined boots on her feet, and a select few winter outfits, including the knit sweater and skinny corduroy pants she wore. Her workaholic Miami lifestyle consumed her. Vacation time went unused, and trips home never happened. Her body and mind needed this respite from obligation.

After zipping her coat, Isabella opened the overhead bin and yanked at her suitcase. It didn't budge. Someone had crammed a too-large bag into the overhead compartment against hers.

How did you get away with jamming this monstrosity in here? The flight attendant should have made you check it.

Her seat partner relocated to the edge of Isabella's seat. She resembled a runner at the start line, crouched for a fast take-off. "Sorry." Isabella pressed her lips into a tight grin. "I'll be out of your way in a minute." She tugged once more with force on her bag, sending it plunging toward her head.

"Duck."

Isabella instinctively obeyed the order barked by the man behind her.

His muscular arm flew out to block the suitcase's

downward trajectory. He wrestled it to the cabin floor.

"Wow. Thanks." Isabella gazed into the twinkling blue eyes of a tall and fantastically good-looking man. He wore an attractive scruff of beard and an engaging smile. A leather messenger briefcase hung across his broad shoulders.

Have I been knocked unconscious? Time traveled into my past? I know this guy. Who forgets their first crush?

Chapter Two

"Nate? Nate Elliot?"

"Yes?" He stared for an overlong moment. "Isabella Lorenzo? I can't believe it. When I found out about this business trip, I hoped to see you again."

"Did you?" Isabella's pulse pounded. His cologne's woodsy, musky scent distracted her. Her mind went blank, except for wishing she'd freshened her makeup with more care.

Nate extended the handle of her suitcase. "Quite a few years have passed since that summer. We were what, seventeen? Fifteen years ago. Wow."

"Yes." Her heart hiccupped over the memories of them hanging out at Fontana's during the summer he lived with Angie and Sal, his mother's uncle. He looked so cute in his apron, standing behind the bakery cases. He charmed all the customers, her in particular, before he uncharmingly left without a word, never heard from again.

After that summer, Sal and Angie lost touch with both him and his mother.

Isabella quit asking them about Nate because she could tell how it upset the couple. When he learned of his trip to Pittsburgh, did he hope to see them again, too? "Thanks again." Isabella took hold of the suitcase handle. "Some selfish so-and-so wedged an oversized bag against mine." She observed redness tingeing Nate's ears and a sheepish look crossing his face. "Oh." Her face flushed. "Don't tell me."

"Yup. I must confess." Nate removed the larger suitcase from the bin. "I'm the so-and-so."

"Oops." Isabella scrunched her nose. "I called you selfish, didn't I?"

"You did." Nate grinned.

She nudged his bag with her toe. "Well, you really should've checked that monster, you know."

Nate's grin turned to a laugh.

His eyes crinkled at the edges, just as Isabella remembered.

Don't fall for his charm. I am not seventeen any more. Get off the plane and keep going.

The antsy seat partner stood, crowding against Isabella in the aisle.

Nate jutted his chin toward the woman.

Isabella rolled her eyes. She filed behind the lovebird couple to exit the plane.

Nate followed.

Her progress halted when her suitcase wobbled sideways. Isabella jerked on the bag, but it remained stuck. She heaved a sigh. "Dang it."

Nate chuckled. "These roller bags have minds of their own. Let me help." His hand covered Isabella's on the handle.

Her breath caught at his touch. *Did I imagine that spark? Did he feel it, also? That...zing?*

Nate stooped and rotated the wheels. "There." He straightened and removed his hand. His gaze locked onto hers, and he winked. "All systems go."

"Oh. Yes. Thanks." Isabella continued toward the exit, trying not to stumble over the sense of his closeness behind her.

"Do you still live here in Pittsburgh, Bella?"

At his use of her nickname, Isabella smiled.

"Or are you visiting your family for the holidays?"

A knot lodged in her throat. *He doesn't know about the car accident.* The crew's bidding goodbye allowed Isabella to skip answering Nate's question.

The pretty, platinum-blonde flight attendant with a knock-out figure and large, doe-shaped brown eyes waved at Nate. "See you soon?"

"I'm looking forward to it, Nina." He stepped aside, and the two engaged in playful repartee.

So, that's how you carried on that bag of yours. Sweet teenaged Nate has grown into a player. I hadn't imagined that possibility.

Isabella hurried through the cold jet bridge reeking of exhaust fumes and entered the crowded concourse. The strong, caramel-nutty-vanilla aromas from a coffee kiosk tempted her to stop for a latte and scone, but she resisted. She sped her pace toward ground transportation, intent on leaving the unnecessary calories far behind, along with Nate-the-Player. Her hurt feelings from the past were better left dormant.

"Bella, wait."

Isabella swiveled to see Nate hurrying toward her.

"I lost you at the gate." He fell into her stride. "I know the flight attendant, and we had to catch up."

I can guess about what.

Regardless of his involvement with "Nina, the flight attendant," Isabella couldn't help but return Nate's alluring smile. *You are still irresistible. Nothing changed there.*

"You never answered, Bella. Are you visiting, or do

you still live here in the Bloomfield neighborhood?"

"Actually, I'm moving back from Miami." *Don't talk about staying with Beth and Owen. He'll wonder why I'm not staying with my folks. I can't talk about my family tragedy while standing amidst strangers in the airport terminal.*

"Hey, Nate." A well-dressed older man waved him over.

Nate touched Isabella's arm. "Sorry. I have to speak with him."

She halted, prepared to relegate Nate Elliot to the shuttered place in her heart where she'd kept him for fifteen years.

Nate offered his phone. "Could you give me your number? I'd love for us to spend some time together."

She hesitated.

"Nate." The man waved once more, this time with more emphasis.

Poor Nate. This guy must be a royal pain.

"Coming, Sam." Nate retrieved a card from his messenger bag. "My number's on there. Call me? I'm in town until Christmas Eve."

Isabella took the card. She appreciated its heavy cardstock and embossed company name of DE Commercial Real Estate, New York City. *Ole Nate must be doing well for himself, based on this spiffy business card.*

She poked it into her handbag's side pocket. "Good luck with your business, Nate. And, Merry Christmas." A sadness encroaching into his brilliant blue eyes rattled her.

"Call me. Please? I owe you an explanation." Without saying more, Nate hurried toward the older man.

Confused, Isabella stared after him. *Explanation? After all this time? Yes, I fell into teen puppy love with you. When you vanished from my life, your disappearance broke my heart. I cried grown-up tears. However, you owe Sal and Angie an explanation before you owe me one.*

Isabella followed signs to transportation and boarded the van for the car rental terminal where the SUV she reserved waited. She placed her luggage in its trunk and settled behind the wheel, reveling in the new car scent. No way would she miss her old one she'd donated for charity in Miami. She'd talked herself into purchasing a new vehicle, a four-wheel drive which would hug the Pittsburgh roads in the wintry weather. If she liked this rental, she'd look into buying a new one of this make.

She entered Beth's address into the GPS system and texted the ETA, along with a string of Christmas emojis. She giggled at the reply, a gif of a cartoon girl dancing the hula with the words *Can't Wait*.

Exiting the parking lot, Isabella set the wipers on low to clear the snow flurries smattering against the windshield. The little-girl excitement over the snow chased through her once again. The possibility of a white Christmas boosted her holiday spirit.

Her mind wandered to Nate. *To call or not to call? That was the question.* He didn't seem her type at this point in their lives. He put out definite player vibes, and she swiped left on players. Why get lost in his damn blue eyes again? *Admit it, though, Bella. You are curious about his explanation.*

She needn't hurry to contact him. He'd be in Pittsburgh until Christmas Eve, which was a week away.

She faced enough complications at the moment without layering him into them. She ticked off her to-do's: shopping for new clothes, purchasing a car, finding a place to live, settling in once the moving van arrived, figuring out a new career.

Whew.

A life reset could be overwhelming if she let it be. For now, she would enjoy the rental car and Christmas with her best friend and her family. She toyed with the car's audio system until she located a Christmas music station. While humming along to "I'll Be Home for Christmas," she couldn't stop grinning. The lyrics no longer applied to her life.

No more being home only in my dreams…I'm really home for good.

Chapter Three

Isabella drove with caution, pleased over the lighter Sunday traffic dotting the interstate heading through Pittsburgh. Her parents' accident transformed her into an anxious driver. She didn't miss the crazy Miami traffic with cars darting in and out of lanes at high speeds.

She exited the Fort Pitt Tunnel onto the Fort Pitt Bridge spanning the Monongehela River. This view of the skyline earned Pittsburgh its nickname of "The Only City with an Entrance." A sense of Pittsburgh pride rose within her. *Mom, your cross-stitch told the truth: "home is where the heart is."*

Her drive through the Shadyside neighborhood where Beth and Owen lived proved lovely, as Isabella expected. The Bloomfield apartment homes in which she and Beth grew up seemed tinier compared to the spacious suburban homes. She passed Shadyside Hospital, where Owen practiced general surgery and Beth worked as a nurse before becoming the nutritional coach at the school attended by their twin girls.

Funny thing about how one fell into careers. Some chased and caught their dreams, like Owen, but others settled for the sensible options, like Beth and her.

While growing up, Beth wanted to be a baker or a nurse. Her practical side went with nursing.

Once he dissected the disgusting frog reeking of formaldehyde in middle school science class, Owen knew he wanted to be a surgeon. He never wavered in his pursuit.

Isabella followed her passion for reading and majored in English, but teaching held no interest. Her strange alignment of recruitment interviews after college led her into marketing. She shone at her job. Yet, if asked when young what she wanted to be when she grew up, would she have answered brand manager? *Hah. Right.*

The dream she and Beth shared as teens kept crowding into her thoughts. They'd loiter over coffee and pastries at Fontana's, talking about opening a bakery-bookshop café together. Their families had nicknamed them Beth-the-Baker and Isabella-the-Bookworm,

Will Beth have interest in going into business with me to open "their" café all these years later? She might be satisfied with her life at the moment. Testing the waters couldn't hurt, though.

"You have arrived at your destination."

Isabella parked in the driveway, shut off the engine, and admired the outdoor holiday decorations of Beth's home. Strings of Christmas lights twinkled through the snow-dusted shrubbery. Icicle lights dangled from the eaves. Small wreaths hung in each window of the two-story house, and a single candle shone from each windowsill. A huge wreath with a festive large red felt bow adorned the front door.

Isabella couldn't wait to see how Beth fashioned the inside into a cozy home using her enviable decorator knack. She always transformed their shared dorm rooms and apartments into comfortable yet designer-stylish homes.

The twins charged coatless out the front door,

pigtails flying. The wreath swayed from the force of the door slamming behind them. The identical girls reached the car, snow dusting the tops of their bare heads. They pounded on her window and screamed her name.

She honked the horn.

They jumped away from the door.

Isabella scooted from her seat. She hugged them and then held each at arm's length. "You've grown so much. Let me guess who's who." She tapped one. "You must be Hazel."

Laughing, the selected girl pointed to the other. "No. she's Hazel. I'm Rachel."

"Got it." Isabella grabbed her suitcase from the trunk. "I bring presents for you girls to place under the tree."

"Yay," the girls shouted in synchronization.

"Bella!" Beth rushed from the house.

"I can't believe I'm finally here." Isabella grabbed Beth into a hug. "I've told the girls I've come bearing very special Christmas gifts." She placed a finger to the side of her nose, the old-fashioned gesture they'd used as girls for sharing a secret.

"Oh, yes." Beth returned the signal. "Very special."

"Do I have to wait to open it?" Hazel cried.

"Until Christmas Day?" Rachel poked out her lower lip.

"I'm afraid so." Isabella laughed.

Together, the girls dragged Isabella's bag into the house, setting the wreath once again askew with the slamming of the door.

"I need another hug." Beth opened her arms. "How could you stay away from Pittsburgh for two whole years? We've seen you once, at the bachelorette party in

Vegas."

Isabella relaxed into Beth's arms. "I'm home now, for good. The girls are both so cute with their red hair and adorable freckles."

Beth laughed. "That Irish O'Sullivan blood passed down."

Isabella grabbed her purse from the car. "Thanks so much for letting me crash with you."

"Don't be silly." Beth shut the door. "Owen and I would not have you stay anywhere else. He'll be home from his shift soon."

"I can't wait to catch up about everything." Isabella slung her handbag over her shoulder and linked arms with Beth.

"We'll have plenty of time." Beth leaned close while they walked toward the house. "It'll be an extended slumber party."

"Wonderful." Isabella's mouth ached from smiling, but in a good-tired way. Her smile muscles hadn't been getting much work out lately.

Beth welcomed Isabella into the home's small foyer, which led to the den. "We haven't finished decorating the tree, so feel free to hang an ornament or two."

Isabella glimpsed the tall evergreen in the den's corner and breathed in its sharp, piney odor. Boxes of ornaments sat next to it. The tree glowed white from its strung lights and its treetop star. "It's beginning to smell a lot like Christmas," Isabella sang. She slipped from her coat and hung it with her handbag onto the foyer coatrack.

"Tonight, it'll smell a lot like cookies." Beth propelled Isabella into the kitchen and waved a hand over the countertops and kitchen table.

"Wow." Isabella let out a low whistle. The ingredients for cookie baking, plastic containers, and countertop ovens crowded every horizontal space. "This will be some cookie baking operation." She sprinkled into her palm a few chocolate chips from an opened bag and tossed them into her mouth, sighing in delight over the gooey decadence melting on her tongue.

"Hey, we need those for baking." Beth clipped shut the bag. "Anna and Kate dropped off their ovens and ingredients earlier. They'll be here in about an hour. Jen's coming, too. Everyone's so excited to see you. I bought everything you texted for your mom's cannoli cookies. We'll need at least six dozen."

"Six dozen?" Isabella repeated the amount in a weak voice.

"You're sounding a little shaky." Beth narrowed her eyes. "You didn't forget your mom's recipe? I'm dying to learn how she made them so dang yummy."

"Yes, I brought the recipe." Isabella backtracked to where she'd left her purse and returned, waving the recipe in the air. "I'm depending on you for help. Baking isn't in my wheelhouse."

Beth snickered. "You mean the kitchen is not in your wheelhouse. Remember, we lived together. I'm Beth-the-Baker, and you're Bella-the-Bookworm. You couldn't take your nose out of a book long enough to switch on the oven."

"Our nicknames were accurate. Speaking of which, I have an idea for us to discuss. Plus, you'll never guess the person I ran into on the plane."

"What idea? And, who?"

"It'll keep until after the cookie baking." Isabella reached for the chocolate chip bag once more.

Beth slapped her hand. "Stop it."

The twins careened into the kitchen.

They reminded Isabella of out-of-control spinning tops.

"Aunt Bella." Hazel tugged her arm.

Rachel tugged her other arm. "Come see your room."

The twins dropped their grasp and ran full-tilt toward the stairs.

Isabella took time to admire the well-appointed den leading to the master bedroom before climbing the stairs to join the girls in the hallway. It provided entrances to three bedrooms and a bonus space with a small slanted ceiling.

"Your room is next to ours," Hazel announced.

"You're across from Daddy's office," Rachel added.

"And there's our playroom." Hazel pointed to the low-sloped ceiling room at the end of the hallway.

Isabella glimpsed in the playroom a row of the historical dolls and recognized Beth's from their childhood. She still had hers, too. Beth and she, along with their other girlfriends, spent hours playing with these dolls. *How easy childhood seemed, compared to "adulting."*

She entered the guest bedroom with its connecting bathroom to the twins' room, breathing in a lavender scent wafting from the diffuser on the bath's vanity. Thanks to the girls, her suitcase awaited her on a luggage rack by the closet. Beth had left a book by one of her favorite authors on the night table with a wrapped chocolate on top. A large teddy bear sat propped against the bed's pillows. It wore a colorful, hand-lettered *Welcome Aunt Bella* sign strung on a ribbon encircling its neck.

"Thank you, Rachel and Hazel." Isabella removed the sign and gave the bear a tight hug. "Teddy definitely passes the snuggle test." She propped it against the lighted lamp on the nightstand before unzipping her suitcase to retrieve two packages wrapped in Santa paper.

"Let me open it now? Please?" Rachel begged.

Hazel echoed her.

Beth entered the room. "Girls, you absolutely cannot open anything until Christmas. Put Aunt Bella's gift under the tree."

Isabella handed each girl her gift. "Later, you two."

Beth shooed them from the room. She looked at Isabella and placed her finger against her nose. "Yes, I remembered about the gifts." Her smiling eyes softened her scowl. "You've gone overboard. These handmade matching nightgowns for the girls and their historical-era dolls must have cost a pretty penny."

"What's Christmas for, if not kids?" Isabella play-punched Beth.

"It's probably their last one believing in Santa." Beth rubbed her arm. "Do you think they know already and are playing along to spare my feelings?"

"I hope not. However, in case that's true, let's make this Christmas the best Santa Christmas ever." Isabella examined the book Beth gave her. "Thanks for the latest Nora Roberts. How did you know I haven't read it yet?"

"I took a chance you'd been too busy." Beth sat on the bed. "Remember how you and your dad loved reading the same mysteries and figuring out the who-dun-it together?"

"Yes." Isabella sat next to Beth, fanning the book's

pages. "Dad introduced me to Agatha Christie, Raymond Chandler, and Dashiell Hammett by my tenth birthday. Mom worried those books were inappropriate for a young girl, but she couldn't pry them from my hands."

Before her sweet memories overwhelmed her, Isabella bounced off the bed and returned the book to the night table. "I better unpack." She unhitched the luggage straps holding the clothes in place. "I have been super-busy. The end-of-year whirlwind at work, the transition of responsibilities to my replacement, and packing for my move claimed every moment of my life until I boarded the plane. Will I have time for a rest before everyone gets here?"

Beth checked her watch. "You can take a quick power nap. I've ordered sandwiches for delivery at seven o'clock."

"Pittsburgh ones, I hope?" Isabella licked her lips.

"Primanti Brothers. What else?" Beth raised her open palm for a high five.

Isabella slapped it. "I've grown to love the Cuban ones, but nothing compares to our french fries-coleslaw stuffed Pittsburgh classic."

"You can take the gal out of Pittsburgh, but…well, you know the rest." Beth laughed. "While we concentrate on cookie baking, Owen will whisk the girls out for burgers and afterward settle them into bed."

Isabella unfolded a garment from her bag. "I don't think the bridesmaid's dress is wrinkled beyond repair."

Beth groaned. "Oh, my. It's so green."

Isabella returned the groan. "It's very Christmas-y, very chiffony, and very, very green. The pockets are cool, though. And, at least Jen's letting us wear our own jewelry to personalize our look." Her thoughts went to the jewelry box in her cosmetic case. *Maybe I'll be ready to wear the necklace.*

"Yes. Jen is a pretty laid-back bride, unlike bridezilla me." Beth opened the closet and took out a velvet hanger. She shook it at Isabella. "You can disagree, you know."

"Yes, but I cannot tell a lie." Isabella kept a straight face.

"Hilarious." Beth stuck out her tongue. "Jen does take the cookie table tradition seriously. Preparing one is always a huge job, but she has her heart set on an over-the-top extravaganza." She arranged the dress on the hanger, sighing. "Have you ever wanted to throttle the person who started this tradition?"

"Who, though?" Isabella unpacked the long, silky navy dress she'd purchased for the rehearsal dinner. "So many stories exist about the cookie table's origin. Mom claimed Italian immigrants brought the tradition to Pittsburgh."

Beth hung the bridesmaid's dress and faced Isabella, another hanger in hand. "I remember her saying, but I've also heard cookie tables started during the Depression when no one could afford the ingredients for a wedding cake."

"Well, no matter how the tradition began, I'd like to throttle Jen for talking me into baking Dottie's famous cannoli cookies for her table." Isabella handed the navy dress to Beth.

"That's gorgeous." Beth took it and placed it on the hanger. "Don't worry about the cannoli cookies. We'll bake them together, and everything will be fantastic. Anyway, it wouldn't be a Pittsburgh wedding without the cookie table."

"You're right." Isabella placed her folded sweaters and jeans into a bureau drawer. "I went to a co-worker's wedding in Miami, and I missed it."

"I can bet." Beth hung the navy dress in the closet. "Does anything else need hanging?"

"That's it." Isabella shut her suitcase. "We'll need to set aside a shopping day before you get sick of seeing me in the same few winter outfits."

"Let's make a day of it. We'll get facials and have our nails done, too."

"Agreed. By the way, since I haven't decided on an apartment yet, I've rented a storage unit to hold my stuff when the moving van arrives."

"You must look at the new complex near us. We'll be neighbors." Beth closed the closet door and leaned against it, studying Isabella. "How are you feeling about moving back?"

"It's the right decision." Isabella wrapped her arms around herself. "I'm hugging myself over it."

"I know you're excited about having no work obligations for a bit. You've said you want to figure out a different career." Beth closed the window shades and switched the lamp's lighting to its lower wattage. "I admit sometimes I daydream about shaking up my life, a bit."

Isabella's ears perked up. *You might be interested in the café idea.* "When we have you-and-me time, let's share some ideas."

"I can't wait. It'll be fun, having our girl-to-girl talks again." Beth folded back the comforter and plumped the pillows, "Don't sleep too long, or I'll sic the twins on you." She shut the bedroom door.

Isabella slid out of her fur-lined boots and crawled

onto the bed. Her thoughts pivoted from sharing with Beth about seeing Nate to the wedding and reception ahead. *Holy Dottie's cannoli cookies. Why on earth, even with Beth-the-Baker's help, did I think I could measure up to Mom's cannoli cookie legend?*

Chapter Four

Isabella awakened to the overpoweringly tangy smell of Primanti Brothers' sandwiches. She splashed cold water onto her face, swooped her hair into a pony, and changed into an oversized Pittsburgh home football team sweatshirt worn over leggings before galloping down the steps into the kitchen.

Her gang of girlfriends swept her into a chaotic reunion.

After rounds of hugs, toasts with bottles of a Pittsburgh brew, and compliments on how they all looked fantastic, Isabella raced to the kitchen table. "Let's eat." She tore into her sandwich with uncontrolled zeal. Her tastebuds exploded with each bite of grilled meat, melted cheese, oil-and-vinegar based coleslaw, tomato slices, and french fries stuffed between two thick slices of soft Italian bread.

"Don't eat so quickly, Bella."

Beth's laughing command, seconded by Jen, Anna, and Kate, did not affect her. Isabella took another huge bite and chased it with a gulp of beer. She wiped her mouth with a napkin, mumbling through it, "You don't understand. I've gone without this deliciousness for two long years."

Jen wagged a finger at Isabella. "That's on you for never coming home for a visit."

"We've missed you living here." Anna handed Bella

another napkin. "Here you go, Miss Messykins."

"It's about time you moved back where you belong." Kate patted her stomach. "But how awful of Beth to feed us these gazillion-calorie sandwiches. We all have dresses to fit into."

Beth surveyed the table. "So, you mean no one will lick the cookie batter or taste-test the results, right?"

A laughing chorus of "wrongs" answered.

Isabella pulled the cannoli cookie recipe out from the pocket of her sweatshirt. She removed the fragile, sepia-toned paper from the baggie and smoothed it out with care on the table. A sweet but pungent old book odor with a hint of vanilla and almond clung to it.

Jen bounced in her chair. "Is that it? Dottie's famous cannoli cookie recipe?"

Anna poked Isabella's arm. "I remember being at your house and seeing your mom cooking away." She held her hand to the height of the kitchen counter. "She stood not much taller than this."

Kate pulled her long hair into a makeshift bun. "She always wore her coal-black hair twisted off her neck." She swished her head to show off the hairdo. "You resemble her so much, Bella, with your to-die-for olive complexion."

"Oh, you guys." Isabella's eyes misted. "I love being told I favor Mom. I promise, though, I will stay out of the black hair dye she loved." She sat taller in her chair. "Thank heaven I have more inches on me than she did."

Beth's laughter faded. "Bella, you're holding family history in your hands with that recipe."

"You're right. I can't believe I've never looked at it closely." Isabella bent her head over it. Within a moment, she gasped. "Oh, no. This writing is almost unreadable. I can make out cinnamon and zest of orange, but I can't tell how much of either ingredient. And, does is call for one cup sugar or one-and-one-half cups? What about the ricotta? I can't tell make out how many ounces of it." Isabella covered her face with her hands. "Why didn't I spend time in the kitchen with Mom? I could have gone over all her recipes with her and asked about anything I didn't understand."

"Bella, you can't blame yourself." Beth hovered over Isabella's shoulder to study the recipe. "I admit these smudges make entries difficult to read. The zest of orange could be the ingredient that set your mom's cannoli cookies apart from others. But how much did she use?"

"Let us see if we can help decipher it." Kate held out her hand.

With care, Beth passed the recipe.

Kate, Anna, and Jen took separate turns studying the recipe, but each shrugged.

"Don't fret." Beth returned the paper to Isabella and patted her shoulder. "We'll figure it out." She snapped her fingers. "The cannoli cookies at Fontana's taste similar to your mom's. You can ask Mrs. Fontana for help with the recipe."

"I could." *What about it, Mom? Should I share your prized recipe with Angie? If it means your legendary cannoli cookies can still be the talk of the Pittsburgh cookie table world, I guess you'd approve.* "Sal and Angie are expecting to see me. Do we have any plans tomorrow?"

"Nope. Our Christmas break doesn't begin until Wednesday."

"Don't remind us about Christmas vacation." Anna elbowed Kate. "After the homeroom holiday party tomorrow, we'll have to keep my Ethan and your EJ occupied for two weeks."

"At least Walt's teaching calendar means he's off to help you, Anna." Kate tugged her eyebrows together, wrinkling her forehead. "Matt has to work through the holidays. That's how a cop's family rolls."

"Oh, Kate, we appreciate our police families." Beth motioned to Isabella. "I'm lucky to have Bella to help me keep the girls occupied while Owen works. He has surgeries scheduled through the end of the year."

"I have to earn my keep, don't I?" Isabella wriggled her fingers toward Kate and Anna. "I must see photos of the boys, please." She spent the next few minutes swiping through the pictures on Anna's and Kate's phones. "They're continuing our tradition of being kindergarten classmates. They'll be the most handsome ring bearers at Jen's wedding, and the twins will be the most adorable flower girls."

"I can't wait for Simon and me to start our family." Jen's eyes sparkled.

Isabella hoped the conversation wouldn't shift to her single life and biological clock. She returned the phones to Anne and Kate. "Your idea to ask Angie for help with the recipe makes sense, Beth. I'll head over to Fontana's tomorrow morning."

"Perfect excuse for espresso and pastry. Yum." Beth licked her lips.

"The best."

A perfect excuse to run into Nate, too? Isabella put both her cannoli calamity and anticipation about seeing Nate again out her mind. She directed her energy to putting Beth's double ovens and the countertop ones to work. Soon the mingled aromas of shortbread, mint chocolate chip, peanut butter, and snickerdoodle cookies hung in the air.

At eleven o'clock, Isabella snapped the top on the last of the extra-large plastic containers, each filled with six dozen cookies ready for the freezer until being delivered for the wedding reception. Her containers remained empty, but she hoped not for long. "I'm ready not to smell anything sweet for a while." She dropped into a chair at the kitchen table, joining the others. "At least not until my trip to Fontana's in the morning."

"Thanks so much everyone." Jen's voice cracked with telltale emotion. "My cookie table will be perfect."

Kate gave Jen's arm a squeeze. "It will be gorgeous and delicious." She leveled her gaze on Isabella. "Bella, do you have a date for the wedding?"

Ugh. I'd hoped to avoid this conversation.

"Your silence says no." Kate clicked open her phone. "I created your profile on Pittsburgh Possibilities, the local dating app. You already have several guys messaging you."

"You didn't." Isabella grabbed at Kate's phone but missed. Nate's face flashed into her mind's eye. "For your information, on the plane I ran into a sort-of former boyfriend. He wants us to get together while he's in town." All her girlfriends' questions mingled together in loud shrieks.

"Who is he?"

"Not Steve, I hope. Isn't he married?"

"Is he someone from Miami?"

"No, he's not Steve or someone from Miami." Isabella's skin prickled. *Why did I open my big mouth?*

"If you must know, I ran into Nate Elliot."

Beth hit her arm. "*The* Nate Elliot?" She grabbed Kate's phone. "Let's check him out."

"Oh, I remember that name." Jen clasped her hands over her heart. "Isn't he the guy you crushed on the summer before our high school senior year?"

Kate frowned. "I don't remember this."

"Me neither." Anna tapped a finger against her temple. "Oh, I know why, Kate. That summer we lived at camp, working as counselors. And nobody told us about Bella's love affair?"

"It wasn't a love affair." Isabella folded her arms, as if in protection against the onslaught.

"I knew she flirted with a guy who worked at Fontana's that summer, but I didn't know anything else." Jen held up two fingers. "I promise."

Beth gave a slight headshake. "He has no profiles on any social platform, but he is on the website for DE Commercial Real Estate in New York City."

Isabella snapped her fingers. "He gave me his business card." She hurried to the foyer to retrieve it from her purse. Returning, she tossed it onto the table. "From the expensive design, the company must be a successful one."

Beth swiped a thumb against the phone. "I'm scrolling through his bio, and it says he went to Harvard."

"Harvard?" Isabella hadn't pegged Nate as an Ivy League guy.

"Yes." Beth rotated the phone to show his photograph. "He's quite a heartthrob."

"Okay, okay." Isabella shushed the group's loud squeals.

Beth returned the phone to Kate. "Bella, spill it. How was it, seeing him again after so many years?"

Isabella took a deep breath before launching into the luggage catastrophe and the easy banter back and forth. She left out the part about the bombshell flight attendant…and, about him saying he owed her an explanation. "He didn't wear a ring, and he acts very single."

"It's settled." Jen clapped her hands sharply. "You must meet with him."

Kate waggled her phone at Isabella. "Unless you want me to match you with one of Pittsburgh Possibilities?"

Isabella slit her eyes toward Kate.

Anna sighed. "It's romantic. It's meant to be. You're calling him, Bella."

Beth placed a hand above the center of the table. "Here's to calling Nate."

Each girl joined in stacking their hands.

Isabella placed hers on the top.

"We shout 'Go Bella' on my count." At the countdown of three, two, one, Beth nudged from the bottom.

All hands flew off. "Go, Bella" reverberated through the kitchen.

Isabella had joined in the fun, but she couldn't stave off her concerns. *Will Nate and I hit it off together? Even if we do, is my life too unsettled for the start of a complicated, long-distanced relationship?* The buzz of conversation about the upcoming schedule for the Friday night rehearsal dinner and Saturday wedding diverted her attention from Nate.

Soon, one by one, each girlfriend departed with

containers of cookies in hand.

After she bid the last one goodnight, Isabella expelled an exhausted sigh. "Bed beckons."

"You've had a long day." Beth pulled her close for a hug. "We're so happy you're here, Bella."

"Thanks. Me, too." Isabella hurried upstairs and tiptoed past the twins' room. She readied herself for bed in record time, saving her shower for the morning in order not to wake the girls. Her worry over baking the cannoli cookies and calling Nate challenged her sleep. Terrifying dreams of burnt inedible cookies and rejected phone calls pursued her all night long.

Chapter Five

The next morning, Isabella shuffled into the kitchen, hypnotized by the nutmeg-cinnamon coffee scent. She found a note from Beth propped against the box of Isabella's favorite cereal.

We're off for the day. Text with updates about Angie—and Nate.

She sipped the Christmas blend coffee from an oversized Santa mug and played with Nate's business card she'd left on the kitchen table. Over her bowl of cereal, she fielded texts pinging from Kate, Jen, and Anna, all encouraging her to meet with him. Somehow, the idea sounded much better in the craziness of last night.

A shower will help me think straight. By the time she stepped from it, she'd decided baking the cannoli cookies required her immediate attention. *Calling Nate can wait.* She dressed in warm, woolen black leggings, an oversized, navy-blue cable knit, and fur-lined snow boots. Digging into her cosmetic case, she pulled out the jewelry box and set it aside. *I'm not ready, yet.*

With her makeup applied and hair blown-dry, she galloped downstairs to grab her coat and purse by the front door. Bundling against the cold brought back so many memories. *How long before I lose a glove? I always ended each winter with a collection of single ones.*

She stashed the recipe in her purse and exited the house. Her breaths created puffs in the cold air. Remnants of snow spottily covered the yards and trimmed the lawn Christmas decorations. No trace of white stuff remained on paved surfaces, thanks to the sunshine's evaporating power. She buckled into the driver's seat and thought for a moment what route to take to Fontana's before heading on her way.

The drive through her old Bloomfield neighborhood drowned her in wistful nostalgia. *I can see you on your favorite park bench, Dad, head bent over your latest mystery novel and your silvery hair gleaming in the sun.*

Isabella arrived at Fontana's Corner Bakery to find no close-by parking spot. She circled the block twice, too frustrated to appreciate the Christmas decorations on the old-fashioned lamplights and in the storefronts. On the third circling, she spotted a sedan leaving. "Bingo." She flipped on her turn indicator to claim the spot.

The car backed out to head in the opposite direction. Before she could swing into the space, a car also heading in the opposite direction zoomed into it. She pressed on her horn.

Out stepped Nate Elliot with his messenger briefcase strapped across his chest.

Isabella allowed herself a moment to ogle him. *Have his shoulders grown broader than yesterday?* She lowered her window, shivering at the rush of cold air. "Hey, you, parking spot stealer."

Nate trotted over, blowing on his bare hands. "Hello. What a pleasant surprise to run into you."

"Nice?" She let out a harrumph. "You stole my spot. Didn't you see me waiting?"

"I didn't. First come, as the saying goes?"

His crinkle-eyed laugh and playful tone robbed Isabella of her exasperation.

The driver behind her blasted his horn.

"That's my cue to keep searching for a space, since you took mine."

"Yeah, about that…"

"Yeah, about *that*. You owe me." She grinned, raised her window, and drove off. In her rearview mirror, she watched Nate head into Fontana's. Anticipation of spending more time with him caused her to miss an open parking space near the store. She circled the block several times until a pickup truck with antlers mounted in the front windows vacated a spot close to the bakery. She whipped into the space, thinking of how the twins would love the antler decoration.

Approaching Fontana's, Isabella observed pedestrians passing the bakery without noticing it. She glanced at the surrounding shops. Their holiday-decorated storefronts shouted, "Merry Christmas." Shoppers streamed in and out of their wreathed doors. *Oh, my. Compared to these other stores, Fontana's resembles a place only a scrooge would enter.*

The door chime announced her entry into the bakery. She welcomed the store's enveloping warmth. The aromas of espresso and fresh-baked goodies transported her to childhood. She breathed in deeply, reveling in the mingled smells of yeast, vanilla, coconut, chocolate, cinnamon, and so much more. She checked out the snapshots of customers, displayed throughout the shop. The one of her at about age five with her parents hung on the wall behind the cash register counter, below the business license.

I miss you being here with me, Mom and Dad. We'd

order the almond-flavored, cream-filled, flaky sfogliatelle pastries and sit for the longest time, visiting with Sal and Angie. Isabella's gaze roamed over the bakery, and the word "shabby" entered her mind. The small, worn artificial Christmas tree looked pitiful. The large, glass pane windows needed washing, and the bakery's name needed re-lettering. The tables and chairs sported the scratches and dings of years of use. *Some Christmas music would cheer the place, along with more Christmas decorations and fun Christmas scenes on the windows like the other shops' displays.*

Sal, Angie, and Nate did not notice her entry. All three remained focused on the papers strewn on the corner table where they sat.

Her interest piqued, she called out a greeting. "Merry Christmas."

Nate raised his head. "Merry Christmas to you." He tipped his chair onto its back legs. A grin spread across his face. "So, you found a parking space."

"Isabella," Sal shouted.

She loved how both Sal and Angie followed her parents' preference of using her full name. Isabella held out her arms for the hugs she knew would be forthcoming.

Sal rushed into them.

She inhaled his cologne, the same her dad had worn.

His short, heavy-set build seemed shrunken a bit. He sported more of a balding pate, but his fringe of white hair still stuck out uncontrolled in all directions.

His embrace whooshed Isabella's breath from her. "I. Can't. Breathe." She wheezed out her words.

After one more squeeze, he loosened his hold.

Angie's hug encircled her next. The old woman's

cinnamon-scented embrace felt like home. Though age diminished Angie's height a bit, her trim figure remained about an inch taller than her stocky husband.

"Coffee and a *sfogliatella* coming up." Sal rushed to get the order.

"Your favorite." Angie beamed at Isabella. "Come join us. Nate told us you two were on the same plane."

"Yes. He helped with my luggage." Isabella took the seat opposite Nate, appreciating once again his movie-star blue eyes, and exchanged grins with him. She hooked her purse to the chair and slid her arms free of her coat, which lodged behind her against the chair's rails.

Sal served Isabella coffee and pastry before taking the adjacent seat. "It's about time you came to your senses and moved back."

"I agree." Isabella took a bite of *sfogliatella*. Flakes of the pastry fluttered onto the plate, and she licked the cream filling from her fingers. "Delicious, as always." She raised the coffee mug and swung it over the scattered papers. "Are you three working on something together?"

"We are." Nate again rocked his chair onto its back two legs and balanced it. "I'm selling the bakery for Uncle Sal and Aunt Angie."

The unexpected announcement soured the pastry in Isabella's stomach. "Selling?" She thudded the mug onto the table, sending the liquid sloshing. "Sal? Angie? You're selling Fontana's?"

Sal busied himself wiping away the spilled liquid before answering. "It's time for Ang and me to retire. We're moving into a retirement center in St. Petersburg, Florida, where Angie's sister lives."

"No more climbing stairs to live above the shop."

Angie's eyes brightened. "That I won't miss." She sighed. "But, having no immediate or extended family interested in the place, we needed to find a buyer."

"That's where Nate comes in," Sal broke in. "One of our customers, Muriel, graduated from high school with Nate's mom, Diana. She's my niece, if you remember?"

Isabella nodded. Sal's references to Diana never smacked of favor. Nate never spoke of her at all that summer.

"Muriel serves on the high school's reunion committee, and this spring they celebrate their fortieth." Sal whistled. "Hard to believe Angie and I went to our sixtieth one a couple of years ago. Anyway, Muriel contacted Diana to invite her, and one bit of conversation led to another."

"Conversations do meander with Muriel," Angie interjected. "She let Diana know Sal and I were thinking of selling, and Diana called us. We talked a long time. She mentioned Nate being a commercial real estate broker, and before you know it, Nate's found us a buyer."

Sal thumped a fist against his chest. "It's brought the family together. And, Nate will take good care of us."

"I will." Nate gave a confident nod.

"It's still going to be Fontana's though, right?" Isabella asked. Their downcast expressions answered. She clenched her hands together in her lap. "So, if this won't be a bakery any longer, what will it be?"

"Something very much needed." Nate landed his chair on all four legs. "You must agree customers find parking an issue."

Isabella's laugh came out in a halfway snort. "Yeah.

You stole my spot, remember."

"Sorry." Nate leaned over the table to jut out his hand. "No hard feelings?"

"We'll see. You owe me." Isabella shook his hand, and the unmistakable zing traveled through her. *No denying it. You, Nate Elliot, have grown into an impossibly sexy man.*

Nate released her hand and gestured toward the shop's windows fronting the street. "Our duel over the parking spot illustrates why my client's offer makes sense. This location will be perfect for a high-rise parking deck."

"A parking deck?" Isabella sputtered the words. "You're fine with this idea, Sal? Angie?"

"I wouldn't say fine, Isabella." Sal placed his hand over Angie's. "But we trust Nate. He says it's the best offer we will get. Our kitchen equipment needs an overhaul. We've barely broken even in the past few years. Our clientele has dwindled to our few loyal customers."

"Our customer base has aged, like us." Angie winked at Sal. "No one wants to purchase the bakery, but the land and location draw interest. Nate's worked through the zoning and everything."

The door chime announced customers entering the store. Isabella noticed these two women fit the aging demographic.

"Hey, Louise. Renee." Angie greeted them.

She and Sal joined the ladies at the bakery cases.

The familiar, friendly conversation Isabella overheard among them warmed her heart until Nate interjected his thoughts.

"Louise and Renee are the perfect example of

Fontana's customer base, which erodes with each obituary. Sal and Angie can't compete with similar, nearby. businesses. They don't have a website, so they offer no internet orders. They have no delivery services. They haven't introduced a new menu item since they opened fifty years ago."

Isabella couldn't counter his caustic criticisms.

"Don't overlook Sal and Angie are in their eighties." Nate folded his arms across his chest. "They don't need the stress of this daily grind. Climbing the stairs to their home after a long day must exhaust them."

"I can agree it could be time for Sal and Angie to enjoy retirement. But, a parking lot? That's the best offer you can bring to them?" Isabella let judgment drip from her voice.

"It's the best financial decision for them." Nate's tone turned critical. "And, they are my family."

Isabella caught the emphasis on *my*, and heat flushed through her. *Sal and Angie are family to everyone in this neighborhood—most especially me, with both my parents gone. You disappear from Sal and Angie's lives, yet you believe you understand what's best for them? Can't you see how their hearts are breaking at the idea of their beloved bakery being razed?*

Louise and Renee departed in a flurry of laughter and wisecracks.

Sal leaned his elbows against the top of the case. "Longtime customers will make it hard for us to sell, Isabella." His voice quavered. "We've been a part of this neighborhood for five decades. When we opened, we were spring chicks. It's been a fulfilling but hard life. It didn't make us millionaires."

"Not even dollar-naires." Angie half-smiled.

Isabella hated to ask, but she knew she must. "What date will you close?"

"We have to sign the place over by noon on New Year's Eve. We figure we'd close the day before. We'll have until the middle of January to vacate." Sal slapped the top of the case. "It's been a good run."

Isabella strummed her fingers on the table, her mind racing. Fontana's being for sale right at this precise moment in her life could not be coincidental. *What if I buy Fontana's and transform it into the bakery-bookshop café Beth and I have dreamed about? It would be a new start for the old place… and, for me.*

Chapter Six

Isabella inspected the shop once more, this time with a more critical eye. Her senses felt on fire. A mental checklist formed.

Repaint. Update the equipment in the kitchen, starting with what's most needed. Change out the lighting and wall décor. Create a website. Offer online world-wide sales of select bakery items.

The upstairs apartment gave her a place to stay until she renovated it into a loft bookshop. In the meantime, she'd create book nooks throughout the store and stock them with used books.

I'll need financial backers, pronto. My savings and inheritance will never be enough, not to compete against the parking lot conglomerate's offer. And, I'll need a product to establish the shop's brand. One that will go viral on social media and turn an immediate profit. But what?

The answer materialized, clear as the view from Pittsburgh's Mt. Washington. *Dottie's Cannoli Cookies. Beth and I must nail the recipe, first, with Angie's help.*

She resolved to keep her idea secret from Sal and Angie until she worked out everything. *If I let them think I can keep the place going only to fall short, I'll be the one who breaks their hearts.*

The parking deck offer expired at noon on New Year's Eve. Would Nate agree to delay Sal and Angie from accepting it until she knew she could buy it? Would he support her or warn her she was shooting for the moon? Those words reminded her of the poster from her childhood bedroom.

What did it say? Something about if you miss, you still land among stars? So, I will shoot for the moon. I will blast off on this adventure, and Dottie's Cannoli Cookies will make lift off successful.

"Sal, Angie." Isabella shifted in her seat to view them better at the bakery cases. "Can you help me? I need at least six dozen cookies before New Year's Eve."

"For your girlfriend Jen's wedding?" Angie bobbed her head. "We're invited. Nate is—"

"Wait a minute, Aunt Angie," Nate interrupted. He lifted a clipboard marked ORDERS off the counter at the register. "You already have quite a few orders. Can you add another?"

Isabella crimped her lips together.

"Of course." Angie's voice raised in rebuttal. "We can fill Isabella's order, without a problem."

"Thanks, Angie" Isabella shot a triumphant look toward Nate. "Do you remember my mom's cannoli cookies?"

Angie clapped her hand to her cheek. "Do I ever. Mine never compared to Dottie's. She said her secret was letting the sun shine in. Do you know what she meant?"

"I haven't got a clue." Isabella fished the recipe out of her handbag. "However, I have her recipe, passed down from my great-great-grandmother. I can't make some measurements. Would you have time to help me? It would mean so much if Dottie's cannoli cookies could be on the cookie table at Jen's reception."

And for sale in your bakery cases.

Angie answered without hesitation. "Let me see the precious document."

Isabella offered it.

"I'll make a copy. We must take care with this original." Angie exited through the hanging door which led to the kitchen, back office, and stairs to the apartment above the shop.

Sal joined Nate again at the table, and he flipped through the conglomerate's offer.

Isabella paced the bakery, imagining it hers.

Angie reappeared and returned the recipe to Isabella. "I handled it with kid gloves. Let's get together tomorrow evening to bake a batch?" She joined Nate and Sal where they sat.

"Thank you." Isabella slid the document into her bag. "I'll bring Beth O'Sullivan, if you don't mind? She's quite a baker and has offered to help with the cookies. Do you remember her?"

"Yes, of course. You and she were inseparable as kids." Angie tapped Nate's arm. "You remember Beth, don't you?"

Nate answered, his eyes on Isabella. "I remember her. She would come here with you and wait until my shift ended."

He remembers. Isabella breathed in sharply. *What else do you remember from that summer? Riding the incline to the top of Mt. Washington? Our first kiss at the observation tower overlooking the city? All the other kisses that followed? Until, one day, you disappeared from my life.*

"By all means bring Beth." Angie dusted her hands together. "The more in the kitchen, the merrier."

The door chime announced an incoming customer,

an older, short man sporting a gray goatee, round spectacles, and books tucked under his arm. His sartorial flare reminded Isabella of her college literature professors. He wore a gray trench coat, a red winter scarf, black corduroy trousers, and polished black Oxford shoes. A seasonal red bowtie peeked out from the coat.

Sal welcomed him. "Good day, Charlie. You're in early today."

Charlie raised a hand in greeting, without turning his head.

Sal nudged Nate. "I bet you remember Charlie, too. The day we opened our doors decades ago, he bought the first pastry we sold. He comes in each day, as constant as the Northern Star."

Nate rubbed his knuckles over his cheek stubble. "Wasn't he always asking for the cookie of the day special and a cup of coffee? His order never changed."

"It still hasn't." Angie's voice wavered. "He brings his books, sits and reads until we close shop. We'll miss him."

"We worry about where the crotchety old bear will go when we're not here anymore." Sal squinted the man's direction. "He lives alone, almost hermit-like, and he loves to collect books."

Angie nodded at Sal. "Go on. Get him his order." She called to Charlie. "We'll be right with you. We're visiting with our great-nephew Nate, and his friend Isabella."

Isabella noticed Angie's clever way of making it seem she and Nate were together. *Who needs Pittsburgh Possibilities?*

Sal placed his stack of papers he'd been reading into

a folder and stood. "Nate, leave these papers for Ang and me to study. There's no hurry for us to sign."

"Why wait, though?" Nate's body tensed. "I think we've covered the details."

"Nate, don't you think Sal and Angie should take their time?" Isabella tapped a finger on the folder. "Someone interested in keeping Fontana's open might make a competing offer."

Someone like me.

"I've heard of no other offer." Color splotched Nate's cheeks. "I see no reason to wait."

"I need to speak to Charlie." Angie stood and rested her hand upon Nate's shoulder. "Give Sal and me more time to wrap our heads around this big decision. How about you join Isabella and me tomorrow at closing time? We'll talk more about the offer while we bake cannoli cookies. In the meantime, you two should go grab a lunch."

Isabella recognized the matchmaking twinkle in the woman's eyes.

Nate raised his hands in surrender. "I've brought a terrific deal to you. I guess reviewing it for a while longer will convince you both." He directed his high wattage smile Isabella's direction. "What do you say, Bella? Shall we grab lunch? I owe you for robbing the parking space." His smile faded. "And, we can talk about that summer."

His last comment tickled Isabella's curiosity. *Are you referring to the explanation you say you owe me?* Before she could say yes to the lunch, her phone vibrated with a text from Beth.

—*Pizza and deck the tree 6:30ish tonight?*—

Her counter-invitation to Nate flew from her mouth.

"I need to get a few things done this afternoon, so how about a Pittsburgh pizza tonight instead of lunch? I'm staying with Beth and her family until I find a place. She'd love to see you again."

"Sounds terrific." Nate scrambled to his feet. "What time?"

Isabella dashed a text off to Beth, holding her breath for approval of the already-extended invitation.

Beth's answer of yes with the time for dinner exploded on the screen with fireworks.

Isabella answered with a heart emoji before addressing Nate. "How about six-thirty?"

"Sounds good. Will you text me Beth's address?"

"What's your number?"

"I seem to remember asking for yours."

Isabella's heart rate ramped up at his irresistible, flirty, crinkle-eyed grin.

He called out the numbers.

She added him as 'Nate the Player' and shared hers and Beth's contact information. His phone pinged, and Isabella swallowed hard. *No takebacks now.*

Nate tapped on his phone for a moment before sliding it into his pocket. "Got it. I'll bring beer." He gathered his set of papers into his leather portfolio and shoved it into his messenger bag. "Hey, Sal. How about some pastries for me to take for dessert?"

Sal rocked on his heels. "You betcha."

"See you tomorrow." Isabella threw a kiss to Sal and hugged Angie.

"Give Nate a chance. At heart, he's a good guy," Angie whispered.

"He seems like it." Isabella smiled. *Time will tell.*

Once again, she wondered about the explanation he

wanted to share with her. She exited the bakery, her stomach aflutter. A waving motion in the window caught her attention, and she realized Nate was dangling one of her gloves. *Losing one so quickly must be a record for you, Isabella.*

He met her at the bakery door. "Does this make us even over the parking space?"

"You wish." Laughing, she snatched the glove. "See you tonight."

"Yes." Nate bowed, making a flourishing hand motion. "I'll attempt to redeem my thieving ways to you. Be thinking of what actions I need to undertake for your forgiveness."

Isabella poked the glove into her pocket and grinned. *I know exactly. Hold off pressuring Sal and Angie over signing your parking conglomerate deal until I can buy it myself. It's a huge ask, but wouldn't you want to protect Fontana's legacy for your family's sake?*

She walked to her car, sensing Nate's eyes following her. Her body responded, overheating as if scorched by the Miami sun. *Zing.*

Chapter Seven

Isabella left Fontana's and drove straight to the independent bookstore with a coffee shop located near Beth's house. She purchased several books on business startups, a pack of colored pencils, and a notebook. Observing the store's layout inspired her to sketch the layout of her bakery-bookstore café. She stared at the dream on paper. Her surroundings faded while her imagination pulled her into the drawing, almost as though it came alive.

A text from Beth asking her whereabouts startled Isabella, jolting her back into reality. The time on her phone told her Nate would arrive in an hour. She sent Beth a return message before gathering her belongings to leave.

—Be there in ten minutes…so much to talk about—

While driving to Beth's, Isabella catalogued in her mind the meager wardrobe pieces she'd packed. *What will I wear tonight for tonight's…well, dare I call it, date?* She pulled into the driveway behind Owen.

Beth met them both at the door, tapping a finger on her watch. "We have less than thirty minutes before Nate arrives." She pointed to Owen. "Order the pizza." She pointed to the twins. "Bath time. Go. Put on your cute Christmas nightgowns." She pointed to Isabella. "Make yourself alluring for your date. We'll talk later."

Isabella raced upstairs. She swapped out her navy

sweater for a long-sleeved, burgundy tunic top over the same leggings she'd been wearing. Checking herself out in the bathroom mirror, her make-up and hair screamed for help. She scooped her hair into the half-up and half-down style that best tamed its curliness, washed her face, and reapplied the light make-up she wore, along with a dash of matching burgundy lipstick. When she returned the make-up into the cosmetic pouch, she brushed against the jewelry box once again. She opened it.

Her chest tightened at sight of the platinum book locket necklace with her first initial elaborately monogrammed on its face. Lifting it from the box, she opened the locket and read the inscription engraved on the inner facing sides. "May all your once upon a times…end happily ever after." She closed it and rubbed her thumb over the words on the back. "Happy 30th. Love, Mom and Dad."

Isabella dangled the long necklace in the air. Like her, it remained closed up for two years. She clasped it around her neck and admired its gleam against her burgundy top. *Mom and Dad, it's perfect. How like you both to have purchased such a beautiful gift early, three months before the date. Who knew I'd celebrate that birthday…those that have followed and are to come…as well as everything else special in my life…without you?*

Isabella plucked a tissue from the box and dabbed her eyes. The locket would be a good luck charm for her business venture. Her ownership of a bookstore-bakery café would thrill her parents.

Will Beth say yes to the idea of their café? Will Nate support it? With those questions swirling in her mind, Isabella rushed downstairs, taking her notebook containing the rendering of the café.

Beth paused in emptying the dishwasher. "You look fabulous. I love your locket."

"Thanks." Isabella touched the necklace, fighting tears.

She told no one, not even Beth, about finding the jewelry box in a Happy Thirtieth birthday gift bag while clearing out her parents' apartment after the accident. It took her months to look inside and more months to open the jewelry box and card. *Somehow, it feels right to wear it now, with my return home for a fresh start.*

Isabella placed her notebook on the kitchen desk. She began setting the table with oversized Santa paper plates. "You won't believe what I found out at Fontana's. And, what I found out about Nate's trip here."

The doorbell rang.

Isabella froze, holding a plate in mid-air.

The Christmas music streaming from the house speakers filled the moment until Beth flapped a hand towel at her. "Earth to Bella. Go let Nate in."

"Oh. Yes, I should do that." Uncertainty over spending time with him attacked Isabella. She finished setting the last plates on the table, stalling the inevitable, until she heard the stomping of the twins' heading to the door, chanting.

"Bella's got a boyfriend. Bella's got a boyfriend."

Isabella ran after them, but she wasn't fast enough.

Hazel jerked the door open.

A smiling Nate stood on the front porch. He balanced a box with the Fontana's logo in one hand and a twelve pack of a popular Pennsylvania beer in the other.

"Hello." Isabella tapped each twin's head. "Rachel. Hazel."

"Love your Christmas nightgowns." Nate offered the Fontana's box to them. "Which one of you wants to take dessert to the kitchen?"

"Me."

"Me."

Nate raised his eyebrows toward Isabella.

"Girls, see if your mom needs help in the kitchen." She took the bakery box and waved the twins off.

They scampered away, their high-pitched voices mingling together.

"He brought cookies."

"He's handsome."

Nate's face reddened. "Thanks for solving that conundrum."

"Don't mind them. They're excited." Isabella wondered if her blushing matched his. She hoped he didn't think the twins echoed her description of him. A burst of cold air reminded her Nate remained on the front porch. "Come in. It's freezing."

He entered to the welcoming hellos from Beth and Owen.

"It's been years." Beth took the beer from him. "Thanks, but you didn't have to bring anything."

Owen peered into the box. "Don't listen to my wife. You can bring us Fontana's any time. I'm Owen, by the way." He offered a handshake.

"Nice to meet you." Nate shook with him.

"Thanks for letting me barge in on the pizza party." He peeled off his coat and scarf.

"Happy you could make it." Beth gave a slight swing of the six-pack toward the coatrack. "You can hang your stuff there. The pizza should be here any minute. You two make yourself at home in the den while

Owen and I put this stuff in the kitchen."

Isabella handed the bakery box to Owen. She took Nate's coat and scarf, inhaling his understated musky, woodsy cologne clinging to both. *I'll associate this scent with you always.*

Nate followed her to the den.

Rachel ambushed them at the den doorway with two fistfuls of tinsel icicles and a shout. "Merry Christmas."

"Oh, you little devil." Isabella laughed, brushing the icicles from her hair.

"You missed one," Nate plucked a strand of tinsel off Isabella's shoulder. His stare held hers.

Why do I feel the earth spinning? How cliché.

He broke the moment between them by draping the tinsel over Rachel's head.

She brushed it off. "You're funny."

"I've been told that before, young lady." Nate strode to where Hazel stood on tiptoes at the tree trying to hang a large round ornament. "Let me help you."

She lifted the ornament high above her head. "I want it close to the star."

"Mine too." Rachel chose a matching ornament.

"Let's do it." Nate lifted Hazel. "You're next, Rachel."

Isabella sat on the sofa and the Christmas spirit settled into her soul. She wanted to drink in the moment's happiness. The room's roaring fire cast a rosy glow. The glittery names sparkled on the white felt tops of the red stockings hanging from the mantel. Her heart tightened at the one with her name.

Nate's ease with the twins deepened her interest about a possible relationship. Since Steve, she connected with no other man enough to even consider marriage and children…until being with Nate again. Their chemistry still sizzled.

Her rational brain kicked in. *Whoa, Bella. What's going on with you? First, you want to jump into buying Fontana's. Now, you're thinking Nate could be the one for you?*

"Down you go." Nate placed Rachel onto the floor. He pointed to the icicles on the floor. "How about adding more sparkle to the tree?"

The girls went to work gathering the icicles from the floor and singing along to "Rudolph, the Red-Nosed Reindeer" playing from the house speakers.

Nate joined Isabella on the couch.

"You're very good with the twins." Isabella positioned herself sideways to face him. "It makes me realize I know little about you, except what Sal and Angie shared after you left that summer. They told me about your parents' divorce. I wish you could have confided in me."

"It's a long story. I do owe you an explanation, but we'll need many dates for me to tell it. And, for me to earn forgiveness from you for snatching your parking space."

Her pulse accelerated. "That could be arranged. Perhaps."

She hadn't a clue how with him living in New York City, but they could manage somehow, couldn't they? *Otherwise, why did the stars align for their lives to intersect once more?* Her rational brain kicked in once more. *Whoa again, Bella. Let's see how the rest of the evening goes. What if he doesn't want me to compete against his deal? What if he's not the kind-hearted, generous guy I remember?*

The ringing of the doorbell prompted Nate to his feet. "Pizza. I'll get it." He headed toward the door, fishing his wallet from his jeans' pocket.

Isabella hurried after him. "You're a guest. Put your wallet back right this instant."

"Nope, it's my treat." He exchanged money for pizza and ambled toward the kitchen, the cheesy-tomatoey-pepperoni odors trailing him. "Anyone hungry for pizza?"

Isabella's stomach growled, as if answering. She needed the fortification of food before approaching Nate about buying Fontana's. She must talk with Beth first, though.

Beth-the-Baker and Bella-the-Bookworm. Can our café become reality, built on the delicious legacy of Dottie's Cannoli Cookies? We must figure out the dang recipe.

Chapter Eight

"We've polished off the pizza." Owen popped a lone, stray pepperoni into his mouth. "Now, for dessert." He pointed to the containers of cookies.

Beth slapped his hand. "Off limits. I need to put them into the freezer, anyway."

Nate eyed the containers. "You must have been a busy baker."

"Yes, for the cookie table at our girlfriend's wedding. She's getting married on New Year's Eve. Bella and I are bridesmaids." Beth gently prodded Isabella's leg with her toe.

Isabella ignored her encouragement. She had no intention of asking Nate to go to the wedding with her. A first date to a wedding, especially one on New Year's Eve, carried significant emotional impact. She couldn't ask him to return for it…could she?

Can I even be interested in a man who has no qualms about turning Fontana's into a parking lot? Maybe Nate Elliot belongs in my past, not my present or future.

"Help clear the table girls, so we can finish ornament hanging." Owen supervised them placing their glasses into the sink.

Isabella stacked the used plates and headed to the garage to throw them and the empty pizza boxes in the garbage. Re-entering the kitchen, she found Beth alone and heard peels of girlish laughter from the den. "I assume the ruckus means they're trimming the tree?"

"Yes. Hopefully the guys are supervising, or the girls will cluster the ornaments at their heights, and the top will remain bare." Beth paused in wiping the table and placemats. "Let's talk about Nate, who's not only quite handsome, Bella. He seems a great guy."

Isabella slapped her forehead. "That's exactly what his Aunt Angie says."

"Angie's matchmaking rivals Pittsburgh Possibilities." Beth stacked the clean placemats and sat at the table. "Speaking of Mrs. Fontana, we've been in such a tizz you haven't filled me in on your day. Will she help with the recipe? And, what did you find out while you were at the bakery?"

"I have so much to tell you." Isabella's voice pitched high with excitement. "The short answer is Angie will help us. We're to come to the bakery tomorrow at 5:30 closing time, to work on the recipe."

"Let me check our family calendar." Beth swiveled in her chair to retrieve her phone from the nearby kitchen counter. After checking, she nodded. "Works for me. Owen can be here for the twins. You said that's the short answer. What's the longer one?"

"The longer answer means I need to show you something." Isabella grabbed her notebook off the kitchen desk and joined Beth at the table. She tore out the sketch of the café and handed it to her. "What do you think?"

Beth studied the drawing. "Our café?" She gazed past Isabella, smiling. "We were so young. We believed we could make our dream come true."

"The possibility might have presented itself."

Isabella explained about Fontana's and Nate's parking lot deal.

"I can't believe it." Beth slapped her hand against the table. "I guess I was wrong about Nate being one of the good guys."

Isabella flinched, and an instinctive urge to defend Nate prompted her reply. "Let's not rush to any conclusions, yet. I'm not sure he realizes how his deal will break Sal and Angie's hearts. He is trying to protect their financial interests."

"But what about protecting their hearts, too?" Beth shook her head. "We must save Fontana's."

Isabella flicked her finger against the drawing. "Here's how we can save it."

Beth stared at the rendering. "Are you thinking what I think you're thinking?"

"Yup. Fontana's is the perfect place for our," Isabella beat a drum roll on the table, "bakery-bookshop café. Its signature brand will be Dottie's Cannoli Cookies."

"A great idea, Bella. We'll need money." Beth waved her hand around the kitchen. "Owen and I have some equity in our house."

"No." Isabella shook her head with vigor. "You and Owen have to provide for the twins. I'm a lone wolf. I have some savings and my small inheritance from my parents I'm willing to invest to chase this dream."

Beth knitted her eyebrows. "It's *our* dream. You shouldn't be the one taking all the financial risk."

"You'll be taking risk enough, by quitting your secure job." Isabella's firm tone dismissed Beth's objections. "What do you think Owen will say?"

"He knows I've been feeling dissatisfied. I do like

my job, but I've lost my spark about it." Beth stared at the drawing once more. "I supported Owen's dream of being a surgeon. He will support me chasing my dream. We're a team."

"You're sure?"

"Are you kidding? Yes, of course he will. If I'm my own boss, I'll have more flexible hours for the girls. And, they will adore hanging out there, like us at Fontana's." Beth giggled. "They can be our built-in labor force." She held her fist toward Isabella. "Partners?"

"Partners." Isabella fist-bumped her. "Now, to find investors, and fast."

"Jen is about to marry the person we can ask for help. Simon is in investment banking."

"Perfect. I'll have to meet with him right away. The conglomerate's offer expires at noon New Year's Eve. Nate's driving hard to close the deal before then, but thank heaven Sal and Angie are dragging their feet about signing."

"Maybe Simon can meet with you tomorrow." Beth starting tapping on her phone. "I'll text him. I know he'll be glad to help us."

"Thanks, Beth. I need to get this figured out. If I can't compete against the existing offer Nate has presented, I don't want Sal and Angie to lose out on it."

"Tricky. Nate won't appreciate you competing against him, will he?"

"I hope he will see how much happier Sal and Angie will be if I can buy them out and keep the bakery open. Nate must've observed how they're struggling over their bakery being torn down. It's been their whole life."

Beth's phone erupted in the wedding march. "It's Simon. I have his and Jen's ring tones set to "Here

Comes the Bride." She read his text and let out a whoop of excitement. "He says tomorrow will be his last day in the office before he takes off for the holidays, wedding, and honeymoon, but he can meet with you at three-thirty if you can make it."

Isabella motioned thumbs-up with both hands. "I will be there with Christmas bells on."

"Mommy. Aunt Bella."

Rachel's piercing yell thrummed against Isabella's eardrum. "Ouch." She covered her ears. "I think we are being summoned."

"Sorry for the screeching. Let me text Simon you'll be there." Beth sent the message and handed the rendering to Isabella. "We better get in there before they have the tree looking like two eight-year-olds and two clueless men decorated it."

"Meaning, it would be gorgeous." Isabella smiled.

"Um, no." Beth wrinkled her nose in disagreement. "While Owen and I put the twins to bed and finish the tree, you and Nate can take a little holiday stroll to check out the neighborhood decorations. You can get re-acquainted and tell him about your idea. If he's the good guy we're hoping he is, he should support you, don't you think?"

"Yes." Isabella used the Christmas tree magnets on the refrigerator door to display the café rendering next to the twins' cut-out gingerbread men and scurried to the den.

Beth pointed to the tree and heaved a dramatic sigh. "I told you."

The twins hung the ornaments low and bunched.

The two men stood by, conversing about what teams would make it to the Super Bowl.

Isabella bit back a grin.

Beth rested a hand on each twin's shoulder. "Girls, hang one more ornament, and it's off to bed for story time with Daddy."

Rachel clapped. "It's my turn to pick the book tonight."

Hazel's face crumpled. "No, it's mine."

"We'll check the bedtime reading chart." Beth flicked her hand at Isabella. "Escape while you can."

Isabella cocked her head toward Nate. "How about a walk to view the Christmas lights?"

"I would enjoy that." He patted his stomach. "It'll help me work off the beer."

Isabella mussed the twins' hair. "Night, you two."

Rachel gathered a handful of tinsel icicles.

"Oh, no. We're out of here." Isabella grabbed Nate by the arm. At the front door, she zipped her coat before tugging on her cable knit hat and her gloves. "Let's see who we'd award best decorated yard."

"I'm in." Nate pulled on his jacket and gloves. His fling of his scarf around his neck emitted the potent scent of his cologne into the air.

Isabella breathed it in, and a warm flush of desire shimmered through her. She opened the door and welcomed the blast of frigid air. *Calm down. It's a friendly walk together, that's all. So, why do I feel this time with him will lead to something more?*

Chapter Nine

When they exited the house, Isabella heard singing. "Carolers!"

The group strolled by singing "We Three Kings." One called out, "Join us?"

Isabella poked at Nate. "Let's do it."

He groaned. "Trust me. You don't want me to sing."

"Come on. Everyone can sing at Christmas." Isabella dashed after the crowd and joined singing "Joy to the World."

Nate caught up with her. "I'm warning you." He sang along softly.

When she heard his off-key voice, Isabella stumbled over words to the chorus. She smiled encouragingly at him while inwardly cringing. *So, you can't carry a tune. You're pretty perfect in other ways.*

At the end of the street. the carolers turned the corner to continue.

Isabella waved them off and looked at Nate, whose brilliant blue eyes sparkled in the street light's glow. A silly smile on his face gave him away. She winked at him. "Look at you, all grins. Aren't you glad you joined the caroling?"

"Absolutely."

His six-foot-plus frame hovered over her five-foot-four one. She would need to stand on tip-toes for them to kiss. *Was this moment heading in that direction…a kiss in the Christmas cold air, under a street light, next to an oversized lighted Santa, with fading strands of "We Wish You A Merry Christmas" in the background? It's as hokey as a scene in one of those Christmas movies. But, I love those movies.*

Nate unwound his scarf and wrapped Isabella into it, using it to draw her nearer.

His smell would cling to her after wearing it, but she wouldn't mind. When her lips touched his, she understood the cliché about fireworks exploding the moment lovers kissed. She didn't want this long, tender-yet-hungry kiss to end.

Nate followed their long kiss with short ones before crushing her close against him. "Who needs a view from Mt. Washington?"

"You remember."

He tipped her chin up. "Yes." He covered her lips with his again.

He held her so close Isabella detected their hearts beating against each other. After a few minutes, Isabella shivered at the cold biting through the warmth of their embrace. She leaned away from his kisses and took his hand. "We should head back before we freeze into a kissing statue."

"I could think of worse ways to go," Nate quipped. He walked in step with her. "Let's play twenty questions, to catch up. I'll begin."

"What if I want to go first?"

"Nope." Nate swung her hand. "It's my idea, so I go first."

She twisted her mouth into a half-pout. "Ask away."

"Why were you living in Miami?"

"My job took me there. I've been working in

communications and brand management since college." She halted in place, deciding to tell him about her parents' car accident. "I moved to Miami soon after their funerals. I needed space to grieve."

Nate gripped her hand, and the brightness dimmed from his eyes. "I am so sorry, Bella. Your mom and dad were the best."

"They were." Isabella forced away the lump in her throat, determined not to lose composure. "My turn. Your business card says your office is in New York. Do you live there?"

"Yes. I rent a small studio apartment, but I'm on the road pretty much all the time. My turn. Why did you come back to Pittsburgh?"

"So many reasons. I became tired of my job and tired of missing my friends. The time felt right to return and reset my life, so to speak." She tucked her arm under his, thinking about buying Fontana's. "My turn. What happened the summer your parents divorced?" She went for more. "Do you have any siblings? Why didn't you say goodbye before you left?

"Whoa. You've asked three questions."

"I should have warned you. I cheat at games."

"Now you tell me." Nate chuckled. He stopped under a streetlight and faced her. "Here's a synopsis of Nate Elliot's life. Like my parents, I have no siblings. My grandparents on both sides are deceased, so I have no extended family. My dad's retired career Air Force. Before I hit ten, we'd been posted at six different bases, the last one near London."

"Oh my gosh, London." Envy gushed through Isabella. "I've always wanted to visit there." She covered her mouth with his scarf. "I'm sorry for interrupting.

Continue."

"Thank you." His lips curved into a half-grin. "I'll fast-forward to age seventeen, the summer my parents sent me to stay with Uncle Sal and Aunt Angie. My mother, Diana, fell in love with a Brit she'd met, Sir Harold Wellington-Walker, and started divorce proceedings. The judge gave me the choice of living with either parent. When I met you, that decision loomed over me. My anger about my mother's cheating motivated me to choose Dad. He saw things differently. He refused to let me live with him. I've not seen him since the divorce."

"Oh, Nate." Isabella's voice broke.

"It's okay. Even before the divorce, Dad involved himself very little in my life."

I can't imagine a dad like that. Isabella took Nate's other hand in hers and drew him close.

"Wow, I've gotten long-winded, haven't I?" Nate cleared his throat. "Back to the shortened version of my life. Diana and Sir Harold didn't want a teenager underfoot. Sir Harold finagled me a place at a boarding school for my senior year. I'd already missed the first week of fall term. At Diana's insistence, Aunt Angie put me on the first plane to London. Sir Harold 's chauffeur met me at Heathrow to deposit me at school, where my belongings awaited me."

He leaned his face close to hers, hungry for another kiss.

Isabella let herself get lost in it.

After a long moment, he pulled away from the kiss but kept her face cupped in his hands. "I'm sorry I never said goodbye. My life careened out of control. Anger filled me up. I didn't see the point of staying connected.

I never knew Uncle Sal and Aunt Angie attempted stay in touch with me. Diana told me right before my trip here."

"I wish you shared with me what you were going through."

He dropped his hands and moved a step away from her. "I was embarrassed. Your family was so loving, and mine was a mess. I asked Uncle Sal and Aunt Angie not to say anything, and they promised. I guess they told you about the divorce, anyway, to try to explain my behavior. But, really, I'm the one who needed to explain, not them. It's haunted me ever since that summer I left the way I did."

He peered out over her head.

She wondered if he was seeing himself as that hurt and rejected teenager.

He shifted his attention to her once more. "I don't mean to play a pity card with you, Bella. My year at boarding school provided me with an unbelievable network of powerful people and a fantastic resume for university. Once I graduated, I attended college in the States."

"Harvard." She detected surprise in his eyes. "Beth searched about you online."

He laughed. "I avoid social media. It's too intrusive. However, in case you're wondering, I've not married nor been engaged."

"Thanks for solving the mystery." Isabella stood on tiptoe and brushed a stray lock of his hair from his forehead. "I'm sorry for all you've been through. What about your mom? Does she live in England with Sir Harold?"

"Oh, no." He smirked. "I guess I haven't been clear

about Diana. She lives in New York City with husband number five. Sam."

"The guy at the airport? He's your step-dad?"

"Yes, and my boss. We both work for Diana. She owns DE Commercial Reality."

So, DE is Diana Elliot.

"She and Sam gave me the Fontana's account, and they're watching me like a hawk. I need to close this deal. It's huge for me, and it's also one of the most sizable for the company for this fiscal quarter."

His obvious resolve provoked Isabella's concern. They continued walking hand-in-hand, and Isabella's thoughts were lost in the clouds of their breath hanging in the air. *My purchase of Fontana's is the solution for Sal and Angie...and Beth and me...but it means you won't close the biggest deal of your career. It also means you won't break Sal and Angie's hearts by tearing down their shop and their home for a stupid parking deck. Isn't that a concern for you and your mom? Are you both so hard-hearted that money trumps family love?*

Isabella hooked her arm through his elbow. "Two more questions."

"Go for it." He stage-whispered, "Cheater."

"I know it's not my turn, but I must ask. Why do you call your mom Diana?"

"Somehow, it fits. She does lack maternal bones."

"Ouch." She understood what he meant, though. *A woman like Diana would be all about the money, no matter what. She's probably slim and well-preserved, dresses in expensive designer clothes, and considers her plastic surgeon to be her best friend.*

When they arrived at Beth's driveway, Isabella faced Nate. "Second question."

"Go for it." He pulled on his scarf she still wore to tug her close.

"What if I wanted to buy out Fontana's?"

"What?" Nate took a step backward, letting the scarf fall from his hands.

Isabella stumbled over her words in a rush to get the explanation out. She finished with her plea. "I'm meeting with an investment banker tomorrow afternoon. Please hold off pressuring Sal and Angie on signing your deal until we know if I can buy Fontana's?"

"I can't do that." Nate planted his legs wide in an assertive stance. "My client and my company are expecting me to close this offer by New Year's Eve. It's the first solo deal Sam has given me. My commission will be fantastic. I'll start taking lead on future projects."

Isabella's stomach knotted. "Nate, I don't think *you* understand." She poked a gloved finger against his chest. "I care about Sal and Angie. I want to honor their legacy. They have been a part of the neighborhood for five decades. To demolish their place will shred their hearts. People with your priorities can't understand, can you? For you, it's about the money. The deal. Not family."

Nate flinched.

Isabella bit her lip, miserable over hurting him with such a careless comment...*even if I spoke the truth.*

"Let me be blunt." Nate's impenetrable stare drilled into her. "There's no way you can compete on this scale."

"I accept the challenge." Isabella's voice reflected the coldness of the air.

Nate crammed his hands into his pockets. "You'll be wasting your time." He spoke with an edge.

"It's my time to waste." Isabella marched toward

Beth's front door. The Christmas lights blurred in her teary vision.

Nate called after her. "See you tomorrow at Fontana's?"

Isabella jerked open Beth's front door, sending the wreath cockeyed. She let the sharp slap of the door tell Nate goodbye.

Beth scurried into the foyer. "Bella, what happened? Where's Nate?"

"Don't ask." Isabella untwined Nate's scarf, and his scent attacked her. She tossed the scarf onto the floor, shoved her gloves in one coat pocket and knit cap in the other, and scrambled out of her jacket.

"Let me guess." Beth took Isabella's coat and bent to retrieve the scarf. She hung both on the coatrack. "The conversation about Fontana's went badly?"

"Very." Isabella marched past Beth and entered the den.

Beth settled by her on the sofa. "I assume Nate's not the good guy we'd hoped him to be?"

Isabella let her silence answer. Saying the words out loud would hurt too much. She studied the Christmas tree, noticing how Beth's magic touch transformed it from the twins' madcap decorating into picture perfect. Neither the tree's twinkling Christmas lights nor the cheery fireplace flames cheered her after the debacle with Nate. She touched the book locket, and it girded her with more determination to compete against him.

"Are you going to tell me?" Beth poked Isabella's arm. "Or will we need Owen to extract surgically from you what Nate said?"

"Clever." Isabella settled herself into the corner of the sofa and covered herself with a Christmas throw.

"However, Owen should join us to strategize before I see Simon tomorrow. I have to find investment money."

You haven't won yet, Nate Elliot.

Chapter Ten

Isabella spent the hours leading to her three o'clock appointment with Simon polishing her business plan. When she arrived at his office, she felt her stomach in her throat. After he welcomed her into his office, a call straightaway interrupted them, giving her time to admire his blond, fit, and handsome appearance. *Jen and you will make a gorgeous wedding couple.*

"Thanks, Chris. You're a lifesaver, especially since it ruins your New Year's Eve. Take care, and thanks again." Simon disconnected from the call and leaned back in his chair, smiling. "Sorry. I have a lot of loose ends to tie up before I'm off for the honeymoon."

"I can imagine." Isabella poured gratitude into her return smile. "Thanks for seeing me." She handed him a folder. "I've created this business plan for a bakery-bookstore café Beth and I have dreamed of owning since we were teens. We want to make our dream come true by buying Fontana's, so I'm here about investment money."

"Ahh, you're looking for angel investors."

"What an accurate name. I do need an angel."

Simon opened the folder and flipped through the pages. "I'll look this over while you enjoy a cup of coffee and homemade Christmas goodies in our employee lounge. It's to the left of our office lobby, by the restrooms."

"Thanks." Entering the lounge, Isabella found a few people enjoying coffee and refreshments. *No way I can manage to eat or drink anything.* After she engaged in polite hello's, she stood at the window and watched the light snow. The swirling snowflakes matched how she felt inside, as though she'd ingested a whirligig.

Right when Isabella believed she would jump out of her skin from impatience, she saw Simon's reflection in the window. He walked her back to his office, where she sat opposite him once more.

"You've put together an excellent business plan, Bella." Simon pulled the café rendering from the folder. "I see its possibilities. Investing your assets means you have skin in the game. You have passion for your idea."

Isabella tipped her chin up. "Beth and I both do." Simon's puckering brow worried her. "I sense a but coming?"

"Yes, you sense correctly. First, your market research is pretty thin, especially considering Fontana's location being so close to the big chain bookstore with the popular coffee shop embedded within it."

Isabella opened her mouth.

Simon interrupted before she spoke. "I know what you are about to say, Bella. Your business will offer a unique neighborhood destination and personalized sense of community, and I agree."

"Exactly."

"However, I must be honest. It takes time to find investors, even one angel investor. Time is what we don't have. Sal and Angie have a lucrative deal before them right now, expiring New Year's Eve. You shouldn't allow them to let the offer before them lapse while waiting for yours, which will take time—or, may never materialize at all."

Isabella nod of agreement came slowly. "You're right."

Simon closed the folder and rocked back in his chair. "My professional advice would be to let Fontana's go. We'll work together in the new year to hone your business plan, search for the right location, and find a special investor, or group of backers. You and Beth will one day open your bakery-bookstore café, but I don't see it at Fontana's." He clipped his business card onto the outside of the folder and returned it to her.

Isabella felt like a tiny speck in the business world.

Simon ushered her to the door. "After Jen and I return from our honeymoon, you and I can meet again and go from there."

She offered a handshake. "Beth and I appreciate your help in making our bakery-bookstore a reality one day. And, I can't wait for the wedding."

Isabella left the building and walked into the light snow. The wet flakes mingled with her tears. *If Jen's wedding hadn't kick-started my decision to move home, I would be in Miami for another Christmas…alone, but in blissful ignorance about Fontana's Corner Bakery being for sale. Not realizing the opportunity existed would have been preferable to knowing about it and having it be out of my reach.*

She jerked open the driver's door and removed her coat, throwing it onto the passenger seat. After she settled behind the wheel, Isabella grabbed a tissue from the box in the console and pressed it against her damp face before starting the engine. A glance at the dashboard clock told her the meeting with Simon ran longer than she'd expected. The snow would slow traffic. She texted

Beth she would arrive late to Fontana's for the cookie baking and exited the parking lot.

The Christmas station grated on her nerves. Since she stomped in from her walk with Nate last night, everything grated on her nerves. Now, she faced letting Nate know he'd been right about her trying to buy Fontana's. She'd also have to tell Beth pursuing their dream would take more time than they'd expected, meaning buying Fontana's would not be an option for them.

The sharp ring of her cell interrupted her silent car ride. *You again, Nate-the-Player. Can't you take a hint? I've been ignoring your calls and texts. Once Angie and Sal sign your deal, you'll be off to New York City. Our paths won't cross again. How stupid of me to let you into my heart. The man you've become is not the man I could love, anyway.*

She admitting feeling sorry for him. He was a guy out for himself because he didn't know any other way to be. She winced, remembering the biting words she'd flung out at him. *It's about the money. The deal. Not family.*

From what he'd shared about his family, her mean but accurate comment targeted his most vulnerable spot. What did he know of family? Of having roots? Nate wanted to seal this deal with Sal and Angie to prove his financial worth to his company and to his mother.

Isabella breathed out deeply, her heart feeling heavy for him. No financial deal could clear within him all the emotional landmines of his past.

When she arrived at Fontana's, Isabella found no open spot to park, as usual. She gripped her steering wheel, aggravated. *You're right about the need for a parking deck, Nate, but you're wrong about demolishing Fontana's for it. Why can't you understand that? Do you have a heart of stone?*

Isabella circled the block, she chastised herself for being so impulsive. She'd raised Beth's hopes, as well as her own. Sal and Angie's expectations would be raised, as well, if Beth let anything slip. *I'll be the one breaking their hearts, not Nate.* She dreaded seeing him gloat.

A spot opened up, and Isabella parked. She exited the car and slipped into her coat. Nate's scent lingered on it. Her throat itched to cry over her disappointment. She stood for a moment to settle her emotions, watching watched the Santa on the corner across from Fontana's. He stood next to his charity collection bucket, ringing his bell.

I am thinking too much about myself this Christmas season. Simon did say we will have a shot at the café, just not Fontana's. Think of those who are struggling over the holidays...and longer. Spread some cheer, girl.

She dug into her purse for a donation, crossed the corner intersection, and stuffed the bills into the collection bucket. Helping others filled her with Christmas cheer. Isabella returned to the other side of the corner and reached Fontana's at the same moment as Charlie, dressed immaculately per usual.

He held the door for her. "Merry Christmas."

"Thanks, Charlie. Merry Christmas to you, too." She noticed a bowtie with the pattern of tiny Christmas trees peeking from his trench coat and the book tucked under his arm, a John Grisham paperback that had been one of her dad's favorites. Its wrinkled spine showed the wear of many readings.

Charlie's after my heart. A man who loves thrillers

and buys used books. He'd continue as a steady customer, if I could keep this place open.

The comforting smell of Fontana's baked goods and strong coffee and the warmth of the bakery's heat welcomed Isabella. She wished a glut of customers would shop at the bakery, not only Charlie. Almost a full stock of the day's offerings remained in the bakery cases, meaning the day would be another unprofitable one.

Beth and Angie sat at one table with the copy of Dottie's recipe and a platter of cookies in front of them. Nate and Sal sat at another with what Isabella assumed were papers for the conglomerate's deal spread before them.

At the sound of the door chime, Sal called out without looking. "Be right with you, Charlie."

The old man tipped two fingers to his forehead in silent acknowledgement.

Isabella smiled. He reminded her once more of Dad, a man of habit and few words unless discussing the plot of his latest read.

Sal pushed from the table and headed to the bakery case. "Hello, Isabella. I didn't realize you were here, too." He gave her a quick hug.

"Bella." Beth talked through a mouthful of cookie. "I think Mrs. Fontana has the measurements worked out."

"Beth, please call me Angie." Angie crooked a finger to call Isabella over. "I think I'm close, but the glaze seems a tad off. Your mom would say there's not enough sun shining in. I wish she would've explained what she meant."

"Me, too." Isabella took a bite of one. The flavor transported her back to her childhood when Dottie's baking filled their apartment with scents of vanilla, almond, cinnamon, chocolate, and orange zest. The cookie's cakey texture smacked of the right amount of butter, sugar, flour and eggs. Overall, the cookie tasted close to Dottie's, but not exactly. "You're right, Angie." Isabella finished the cookie before adding, "It's a tad off, somehow."

"How about it, Nate?" Angie carried the plate of cookies to Nate and placed it on the papers. "Give one a go?"

Nate deposited his pencil behind his ear and grabbed a cookie. "Thanks." He finished the cookie in two bites. "Delicious." With his eyes on Isabella, he devoured a second one before speaking again. "I've been trying to get in touch with you, Bella."

Isabella shifted her glance from his, not answering.

Angie swiveled her head between the two and frowned. She started toward the kitchen. "Come on, Beth. Let's whip together another batch. This time, we'll add more orange zest in the glazing."

Beth followed Angie but looked back at Isabella. She mouthed, "What happened?"

Isabella shook her head in defeat. She assumed from Beth's silent questioning their idea remained between them…and, unfortunately, Nate.

Beth mouthed again, "Damn."

Isabella agreed with the one-word curse. However, she knew Beth would take heart in Simon believing in their business plan. *We'll take a win where we find it.*

She passed Nate on her way to the kitchen.

He caught her hand. "Can we talk, Bella?"

Isabella disengaged from his touch. She assumed he would want to continue their conversation from the night before. She wasn't ready to watch him crow.

"Please? Sit for a minute?"

Isabella's gaze roved over the papers. "Is the sale final yet? When do the bulldozers arrive?"

"Sale? Bulldozers?" Charlie echoed her.

Realizing she spoke loud enough for the old man to hear, Isabella pursed her lips in dismay.

"What does she mean, Sal?" Charlie's voice rung out with agitation. "Are you selling? Are they bulldozing the place?"

"Isabella, let Charlie try a cookie." Sal poured Charlie a cup of coffee. "Your coffee and cookies are on me today. Let's sit for a spell, so I can explain."

Isabella snatched the plate of cookies and spun on her heels from Nate to join Sal and Charlie at their table. "I'm sorry I opened my big mouth, Sal. It wasn't my place to speak about your business."

"The news was bound to get out sooner than later." Sal smiled weakly. "Nate told me you wanted to buy the place yourself, but it would be impossible for you to raise the money."

"He did, did he?" Isabella cut a nasty look toward Nate. She pushed the plate of cookies toward Charlie. "Charlie, try a cannoli cookie. What do you think?"

Charlie took a bite of one, holding a napkin under his mouth as if he feared crumbs would fall into his goatee.

Sal tugged an earlobe and squinted his eyes at Isabella. "Ang and I would have preferred to sell Fontana's to you. I know your bakery-bookshop café would be a success. Beth described what you had in mind for the place."

Great. So both Nate and Beth ran their mouths, and

now I've disappointed Sal and Angie.

Isabella snatched her business plan folder from her handbag and flung it onto the table. "I am overflowing with ideas, but I can't raise the cash I need to counter the deal Nate has for you." Without looking at Nate, she added, "You should take it, Sal." An involuntary shudder ran through her. *I can't believe I said that.*

Charlie finished the cookie. "Very tasty." He tapped his finger on the folder. "Will someone tell me what's going on? Do I understand correctly Fontana's will become a parking lot?"

"Let me explain." Nate joined them, taking the seat across from Isabella. "Once you hear about the deal I've brought to Sal and Angie, you'll see it's an opportunity they can't pass up."

"Excuse me. I'm needed in the kitchen." Isabella rushed from the table, trying to block out Nate's sales pitch. *Damn you, Nate Elliot, and your stupid deal.*

Chapter Eleven

Isabella slammed her hand against the kitchen's swinging door, and it smacked open against the kitchen wall.

Beth snapped her head up. "Whoa, that's some entrance."

Angie paused in stirring the contents in a stainless-steel mixing bowl. She handed the spoon to Beth and wiped her hands on her apron. "This dough needs a minute more stirring before it goes into the refrigerator to set. We'll need to grate an orange for more zest." Angie faced Isabella. "I'm so sorry about you wanting to buy our place. We had no idea."

Beth waved the spoon in the air. "I didn't say a word until Nate did." A glob of cookie dough threatened to fall, and Beth stuck the spoon back into the bowl.

Angie nodded. "She didn't. Nate told us about you wanting to counter his deal." She pressed a hand to her bosom. "Sal and I are heartsick about the two of you falling out over it. We don't know what to do. If we sign Nate's offer, we hurt you, and if we wait for you to raise the money to buy us out, we hurt him."

"Oh, Angie. It's too much of a gamble for you and Sal to reject the offer from Nate's client in order to wait for me. I want you to do what's best for you two. Nate and I are fine, so don't worry about us." Isabella forced her voice to remain calm even though anger toward Nate bubbled inside her.

"Are you sure, Isabella?" Concern clouded Angie's eyes.

"Yes, one-hundred-per-cent sure. Blink away your worried look." Isabella removed her coat and hung it and her purse on a hook by the back door leading to the alley. She put both hands on Angie's shoulders and gently spun her to where the recipe lay on the counter. "Now, let's get back to these cannoli cookies. Any ideas about how to tweak the glaze?"

Angie shook her head. "It's something about the orange flavoring."

"If I'd been at Mom's elbow in the kitchen. I would have learned all her little secrets." Isabella began drying the cups Beth washed. "Instead, I preferred spending the time with Dad, discussing the latest book we were reading together."

"Don't be hard on yourself, Isabella." Angie retrieved the dough from the refrigerator. "Not every girl is interested in baking, and there's nothing wrong about that." She dolloped the dough onto the cookie sheet.

"I regret it, though." Isabella scooped a tad of the dough into her mouth. "Yum."

Beth helped herself to a spoonful. "I have an idea. We can sell the refrigerated dough for people enjoy them hot from the oven." She grinned. "Well, people other than Isabella."

"Ha. Ha." Isabella scrunched her face. "You're right, though. We'll offer Dottie's Cannoli Cookies refrigerated dough." She envisioned the commerce website she'd build. The cookies and the dough would be their brand item, along with the other bakery delights they'd produced. Of course, books and gifts would round out their inventory.

Angie placed the cookie sheet into the oven and washed her hands. "I must help Sal with our close-up routine. The gal from the church down the street will be here to get the leftovers for the homeless shelter." She handed the oven mitts to Isabella. "When the oven dings, take the cookies out, let them cool a bit, and glaze them."

"Oh, no." Isabella tossed the mitts to Beth. "That's why she's here."

"You're not getting off so easily, young lady. You're a part of this adventure, so buck up." With a laugh, Angie disappeared through the kitchen door into the shop.

Beth threw the mitts back to Isabella

Isabella caught them, placed them onto the counter, and sat at a stool to watch Beth grate the orange for the glaze. "I hate Angie and Sal are so upset, thinking they've disappointed me when the reverse is true. Nate's out there, advocating for the parking deck deal, and I have to pretend I support him."

"How infuriating." Beth pressed harder on the grater, and the orange spun from her grip. "Oops."

Isabella absentmindedly rolled it back.

"Thanks." Beth added the zest to the powdered sugar and almond extract to create the glaze. "Did Simon say anything other than forget about Fontana's?"

"Yes." Isabella dipped a pinkie into the glaze and sampled it. "I think you need more zest."

"Okay." Beth sprinkled more zest into the bowl and stirred. "Tell me what Simon said. The suspense is killing me."

"Oh, sorry. I have great news. Simon believes our bakery-bookshop café has an excellent chance of getting backers. He wants to meet with us again after their honeymoon."

Beth placed the spoon on the counter and clapped. "What good news. It's so sad we can't take over Fontana's, but we stepped in too late."

"Yes. I let my imagination run away, didn't I?" At the sound of the oven's timer, Isabella pulled on an oven mitt. "I'll get them." She slid out the tray and placed it on a trivet by the bowl of glaze.

After a minute of cooling, Beth glazed the cookies. She scooped one onto a spatula. "Here. Fingers crossed."

Isabella took a bite and gave a thumbs down. "It's still missing something."

Sal entered the kitchen with his nose upturned. "I smell more cannoli cookies."

Nate trailed behind him with a stack of Fontana bakery boxes in his arms and placed them on the counter.

"Charlie's gone, so we can close." Sal grabbed a cookie and devoured it in a single bite. "That's better than the other batch." He tapped the top box. "I packaged the others with our daily leftovers for the church."

"May I?" Nate posed a hand over the cookie tray.

Beth offered him one on the spatula. "Go ahead."

After a bite, Nate licked his lips. "Delicious."

Isabella stalked past him to toss the rest of her cookie into the garbage. She glared at Nate. "You know, you're not a fair judge. You never tasted my mom's."

"True." He spoke through a mouthful of cookie. "But they're still the best cannoli cookies I've ever eaten."

"How many have you ever eaten?" Isabella retorted.

Nate bowed his head. "Touché."

Angie joined them. She tasted a cookie and pursed

her lips. "Hmm, the glaze lacks Dottie's pizzazz."

Isabella pushed the tray toward him. "Sal, you can give these to the church, too." She read over the recipe once more. "We're missing Dottie's oomph. Tomorrow, we'll keep trying."

"You'll figure it out." Sal opened a box and added the cookies.

"We will." Beth gathered her belongings. "I've got to get home. What about you, Bella?"

"You go on." Isabella picked up the empty cookie pan. "I'll stay and clean up."

"No need." Angie took the pan from her and placed it in the large sink. "Sal and I can manage."

"I'll help." Nate walked over to the sink and gently nudged Angie. "You and Uncle Sal go to bed. Bella and I have got this."

Beth sidled next to Isabella and whispered, "You two got this."

"We've got nothing," Isabella whispered back, guiding Beth toward the kitchen door.

"I'm going. Quit rushing me." Beth wriggled her eyebrows. "You two have fun together."

"Aren't you funny." Isabella gave Beth a push, and the swinging door flapped shut behind her.

"I keep the close-of-day tracking sheets in here." Sal placed an opened three-ring binder onto the work counter. "I've got a binder for each year the bakery's been open."

Nate darted a side glance to Isabella.

She realized Nate saw Sal's manual record keeping as one more old-fashioned business technique marking its decline. *With my computer savvy, I could revamp Sal's methods and track everything with accounting and inventory software plus spreadsheets. I could turn around Fontana's.*

Sal opened the binder to the section for that day. He'd entered the meager sales on the accounting ledger. The bottom line showed red. He flipped to the next sheet. "Here's the check- off sheet for the closing procedures. Be sure to turn off all appliances and disinfect everything. I've locked the bakery entrance, so the church volunteer will knock at the alley door to collect the food donations. When you're done with all the tasks, leave the same way. The door will lock behind you."

Angie pecked Isabella on the cheek. "Thank you for helping. Goodnight, and sweet cannoli cookie dreams."

"Night, Angie. Night Sal." Isabella waited until the couple disappeared upstairs before grabbing aprons from the drawer. She looped one over her head and another over Nate's, trying to ignore how his mussed hair added to his sexiness.

"I'll tie you." He stepped behind her and yanked the apron ties to pull her close. "Tell me if I get it too tight."

His words tickled Isabella's ear. Against her will, desire pulsed deep within her. *Step away. Now.* Isabella reached behind her to grab the apron's sash and pivoted to face Nate. "Once we've gathered the dirty items into the sink, you'll wash. I'll dry."

"Aye-aye, Captain." Nate gave a mock salute.

"Very funny." Isabella deftly tied her apron.

He tied his and sprang into action, humming "Rudolph, the Red-Nosed Reindeer."

Despite her irritation, Isabella couldn't help but catch his infectious Christmas cheer. She let herself lean into enjoying his company and sang along to his humming. By the fourth iteration, Isabella swept her arms across the spotlessly cleaned kitchen and elongated the last syllable of the song's last word, "his-tor-eeeeeee."

Nate joined in, belting out the word.

"Ouch." Isabella grimaced before bursting out with laughter. "You're right. You can't carry a tune, Nate."

He leaned against the kitchen counter and crossed his arms. "I told you so the night we caroled."

"You told me quite a bit that night." Isabella's smile dimmed. "By the way, I still have your scarf. I need to return it."

"No rush. I'll visit Pittsburgh often next year." He smiled his crinkle-eyed grin. "We can spend time together, playing more twenty questions and singing more songs." He bellowed out the last line of "Rudolph."

Isabella's body tensed. "We won't spend time here at Fontana's. It's going down in history because of you."

"You're not being fair, Bella." Nate splayed his hands out. "If Uncle Sal and Aunt Ang don't want to sign with my client, they can pass. I'm not holding them hostage."

"Aren't you? Emotionally?" Isabella's voice sunk low, not wanting the argument to carry to the apartment above. "They're not stupid, you know. They can tell closing this deal means so much to you. They love having you and Diana back in their lives. They'll do what you tell them to do, for the sake of family. But I guess you don't understand the meaning of family."

Nate winced.

Isabella pressed a palm over her mouth. Again, she blurted out such an unkind statement, after he trusted her with sharing the pain of his upbringing.

"Perhaps I don't have your insight into family,

Bella. But, I am not controlling Sal and Angie." Nate punched a balled fist into his other hand's opened palm. "I have presented an offer for them to consider. It's a fantastic amount of money for them."

"It's a fantastic commission for you, Nate." Isabella infused her words with a biting tone.

"You believe I care only about the commission?"

Isabella nodded. "You have been crystal clear with me about your motivations."

"What are your motivations, Bella?" He took a step toward her and then backed away. "Even if you could put together an offer, we both know it wouldn't touch the conglomerate's, with their deep pockets. Would you want Uncle Sal and Aunt Angie to take less in order to make your dream come true? Wouldn't that be selfish of you?"

Her heart twinged, as if he'd drawn a bow and sent an arrow plunging into it. She swayed on her feet until anger stiffened her spine. Moving at lightning speed, she wriggled into her coat, shoved her phone into its pocket, and grabbed her handbag, noticing it no longer contained the business plan folder. *It will be safe on the table where I left it. I'll get it tomorrow. Right now, I need as much space as possible between Nate and me before I completely lose control.*

"Wait, Bella." Nate extended his hand. "Can't we work through this?"

"No. You've been clear about your priorities. Money and success, not heart." She opened the back door. "The church volunteer will be here soon for the boxes of leftovers. Be sure you complete the checklist and shut off the lights. The darkness is your friend, isn't it?"

Anne Armistead

Isabella stepped into the alley, her heart pounding.

Chapter Twelve

Isabella tossed all night, her heart hammering with anger over her argument with Nate. When her phone's wake-up alarm beeped, she groaned. With shut eyes, she brushed her hand over the nightstand to locate it. Instead, she sent the stack of apartment guides scattering to the floor. *Good morning, Bella. Great way to start the day. Exhausted and making a mess.*

She threw back the comforter and scrambled to her feet. Her mind and body called out for a workout, to stretch out the kinks and improve her crabby outlook. She changed into a yoga outfit and used the playroom for exercise space. The workout she found on a cable network channel lifted her mood.

After a shower, a bowl of instant oatmeal, and two cups of coffee, she dressed and took off to tackle her day of apartment hunting. While driving from one appointment to the other, she replayed again and again her confrontations with Nate. *We can never be in a relationship. So, why can't I shake my attraction toward you?*

None of the apartment complexes Isabella visited met her checklist of must-haves except for the newer one Beth mentioned. Her thoughts shifted to the apartment above Fontana's…and to Nate.

Stop torturing yourself. You are, as the saying goes, a day late and a dollar short on that business venture.

Quit thinking about Nate, too. He'll be out of your life again before the ink dries on the parking lot deal.

****

Beth and the twins arrived home after school with fixings for tacos, and Isabella joined in the dinner preparation, glad to be distracted from thinking about apartments…and Nate. However, when they left the twins with Owen to head to Fontana's, Isabella's thoughts returned once more to Nate.

"Bella, you look grumpy, like the twins after a sleepover." Beth puckered her face.

Isabella laughed. "I look that out of sorts?"

"Uh, yeah."

"Sorry." *Keep your thoughts about Nate to yourself, Isabella. Nothing will come of talking about him.* "I'm frustrated about the apartment. I love the complex near you. But I must wait until March for a unit. I hate to impose by staying with you so long."

"Don't be silly." Beth dismissively waved. "We love having you. No worries."

"Thanks so much. I'll owe you dinners for a year."

"No, but I never turn away cooked meals."

Isabella snorted a laugh. "I bet."

The traffic light at the intersection by Fontana's turned red.

She braked and looked Beth's way while waiting for the green light. "Don't take what I am about to say the wrong way. I love being at your place, but I can't wait to get settled."

"I completely understand." Beth motioned to an open parking space in front of Fontana's. "Look at that. A space waiting for us is a good luck charm. We'll nail your mom's recipe tonight."

"I hope so." Isabella swung into the space and exited the car.

Beth jumped out and pointed to a deteriorating building at the end of the street. "That structure has been an eyesore for several years. It needs tearing down, not Fontana's."

Isabella stared at the building for a second. "Why couldn't Nate have worked out a deal between its owner and his client?"

Beth stamped her foot. "My thoughts exactly."

Isabella followed Beth into Fontana's and noticed Charlie sitting at his table with several cardboard boxes at his feet brimming over with books.

Nate was poking through them. He looked up. "Charlie's brought a great stash of thrillers. Come look."

She didn't respond to his testing the waters between them. *It's pretty frigid.*

"Be pleasant, Bella," Beth whispered from the corner of her mouth. "Hey, you two."

Isabella ignored Nate and greeted the older man. "Hello, Charlie. What are the books for?"

"They're for you." He tugged at his bowtie. A pattern of Christmas ornaments dotted it. "It's for the bakery-bookshop café idea you have. Sal told me about it. I need to thin out my bookcases. I thought you could use these to test-market your book nooks."

"I like the way you think, Charlie." His comment reminded Isabella of her missing folder.

Has Sal put it some place? She'll have to remember to ask him.

Isabella showed Beth one of the books.

"Oh." Beth placed her hand on her heart. "You and your dad loved that author."

"I see lots of memories here, Charlie." Isabella replaced the book into the box, continuing to ignore Nate. "Did you ask Sal if organizing book nooks would be okay?"

"He did, and I agreed." Sal appeared with coffee and a plate of cookies. "Ang has already baked another batch of cannoli cookies. She said she put more orange zest in the glaze."

Isabella pushed her hat and gloves into her coat pocket, slid it off, and hung it with her purse on the back of a chair at the table next to Charlie's. She recognized the papers for the parking lot deal strewn on it. She assumed the paperwork sported Sal and Angie's signatures. Her hand traveled to the book locket she now wore daily. *It's okay. Our dream will come true, but not here.*

Sal placed the plate of cookies in front of Charlie. "Everybody try one."

"With pleasure." Nate sat by Charlie. He tipped a cookie Isabella's way. "I'm becoming addicted to cannoli cookies."

You can stuff your charm down your throat with that cookie. Isabella repressed a giggle. *Wow, since when I have become so vicious?*

After finishing a cookie, Charlie patted his mouth with his napkin before selecting another. "Tastes better than yesterday's, which were mighty fine themselves. What do you think, Nate?"

With his mouth full, Nate managed a mumbled, "Agreed."

After one bite of hers, Beth shook her head. "These still don't have Dottie's special flavor."

Isabella finished hers before wrinkling her nose.

"They're better but still missing the special Dottie's Cannoli Cookie flavor." She patted her stomach. "I'm going to rival St. Nick in size before we get this recipe figured out."

"You don't have to worry." Nate's gaze swept over Isabella.

Her cheeks heated. *I'm not falling for your flirting, Nate-the-Player*.

Charlie tugged on his belt buckle. "I'm already a notch out from where I've been."

Isabella grinned at him. "The sacrifices of a taste-tester." She tapped her foot against a box. "I can't wait to arrange the book displays."

"You work on that, Bella." Beth headed to the kitchen. "Angie and I will keep on our baker's hat."

"You two will figure out what's missing. I know it." Isabella hoped she projected confidence, but uncertainty gnawed at her. What if they never determined her mom's special ingredient? She knelt by the boxes to look through the books before rocking back on her heels. "Charlie, have you sorted these by author?"

"Yes, and I also have them in order by publication date." Charlie ran a hand over his goatee. "They're mostly thrillers and mysteries. I'll help you set them out?"

Sal leaned over a box before straightening up. "I'll help too, Isabella. Business has been slow today. I'll close early."

Isabella checked the bakery cases, and disappointment rippled through her. The almost full contents meant few customers. She glanced out the store's windows fronting the street. Pedestrians bustled by on the crowded sidewalks, without anyone glancing into the bakery.

Would I, if Fontana's wasn't a special place from my childhood? I bet the ones who came in today are old pals, like Louise and Renee. The place certainly does not ooze a holiday welcome to entice passers-by to come in.

Sal clapped Nate on the back. "Lend us a hand, nephew?"

"Happy to. I've picked out a few I want to buy. I can be Isabella's first sale."

Isabella suppressed a sarcastic *whoopee*.

Nate gathered the documents from the adjacent table. "Let me get rid of all these papers."

Isabella watched him slide them into his leather portfolio. *Too bad you don't mean literally get rid of them.* The folders reminded her about her lost one. "Hey, Sal, have you seen my folder? I left it on the table yesterday."

"Nope, I haven't seen it. What about you, Nate? Charlie?" Sal asked.

"I last saw the folder on the table where you left it, Bella." Nate closed his zipper portfolio and pointed it toward Charlie. "Charlie, didn't I ask you to return it?"

Charlie shook his head, his mouth too full of another cannoli cookie to answer.

Isabella stared at the table where she'd last seen it. "That's weird."

Nate shoved his portfolio into his messenger bag and crossed the shop to place it on the shelf under the cash register. He walked back and stood by Isabella. "I'll help you look for it."

Isabella turned her back against him.

He whispered in her ear. "Am I invisible?"

She swatted the air by her ear, as if he were an

annoying bug.

He laughed.

She didn't.

The missing folder bugged her. *Thank heaven for my digital OCD behavior. I'll find the business plan document in my backups on the Cloud. Too bad about the rendering, though. I'll have to re-draw it, and this time I'll scan and save it, too.*

Isabella surveyed once again the bakery's bleak atmosphere and the almost full bakery cases. *I will not let this place's storied history end with a whimper. It has to close with a bang.*

"You know what this place needs?" She answered her question. "A Christmas makeover. We'll transform Fontana's into a jolly place for its last few days." Before the men could react, she darted into the kitchen. "Hey, Angie. Will it be okay if I give the place a little more Christmas cheer?"

"That would be nice, dear," Angie answered without glancing up from her measuring.

"Are you sure you don't want to help us out in the kitchen instead?" Beth mimed throwing an egg Isabella's way.

"Don't you do it." Isabella pretended to dodge. "You two keep the cookie samples coming while I perform some holiday magic." She scooted back into the bakery and rolled the sleeves of her sweater. "Let's get to work, guys." Isabella crooked a finger at Nate. "You, too, Mr. Elliot."

Nate rolled his sleeves. "Tell me what to do, Miss Lorenzo."

Chapter Thirteen

Isabella organized the work flow, and the four set to transform Fontana's under her direction. The time flew by against the backdrop of Christmas music playing through a Bluetooth speaker attached to Isabella's phone and the aroma of cannoli cookies drifting from the kitchen. She ordered Chinese takeout to sustain their energy, supplemented by successive batches of cookies, each still lacking Dottie's special flavor.

With Nate's help, Isabella washed the inside and outside of the expansive front and side window panes of the store until they sparkled.

Sal and Charlie polished the deep interior wooden window sills until the wood gleamed.

Together, they unpacked the paperbacks and displayed them in stacks on the sills, arranged alphabetically by authors.

Leaving the three men to finish the last of the book display, Isabella grabbed her coat and purse and headed to the hardware store across the street. She purchased paint brushes, acrylic paints in Christmas colors for the windows, and buckets of yellow, white, and blue quick-dry chalk paint for the furniture.

When she returned, Isabella put Sal, Charlie, and Nate to work repainting the tabletops white, chair ladderbacks blue and legs yellow before she walked outside to study the display windows. She tapped into her artistic talents to paint on the windows a Christmas tree and a fireplace with stockings hanging from its mantel. For a finishing touch, she painted a small stool by the fireplace. On it she painted a platter of cannoli cookies, a glass of milk, and a note reading, "Dear Santa, Enjoy Dottie's Cannoli Cookies." She stepped back to view her work and nodded, pleased with her efforts. *Voila. Now Fontana's has curb appeal matching the other stores. Let's see shoppers pass us by now.*

Isabella headed into the bakery, rubbing her almost-frozen hands together. The furniture they'd re-painted furniture looked so welcoming. "Can you guy finish the rest of the pieces while I run another errand?"

Sal answered, his paintbrush poised in midair. "No problem." He took Nate's paintbrush. "Go with her."

"No, I'm fine." Isabella grabbed her purse and tugged on her gloves. "I'll be back soon."

Nate joined her outside the bakery door and let out a long whistle of appreciation over the decorated windows. "You did a fabulous job, Bella."

She replied to his compliment in a frosty tone. "Thanks. I'm glad you approve."

He tossed his scarf around his neck.

Isabella caught the familiar whiff of his cologne. She still possessed his scarf from the night they caroled…kissed…argued. The confrontation still stung her heart.

Nate bent his elbow, inviting her to link her arm with his. "I hoped my hard work would encourage you to speak to me again."

Isabella ignored him. She traveled the sidewalk by him in silence, noticing how their breaths showed in puffs against the cold air. *Like the night we caroled…the night you broke my heart…again.*

She focused on the shimmering of the Christmas tinsel draped on the sidewalk streetlights and listening to Christmas carols playing from the street's speakers. When they reached the Christmas tree lot, the scent of evergreen and the excitement of families choosing their trees disarmed Isabella's anger enough for her to drop the silent treatment. "Thank you for helping."

He responded with his crinkle-eyed smile. "Truce?"

Why not? It's the Christmas spirit, not Nate, thawing my heart.

"Truce. For now." She selected evergreen garlands draped on the wooden lattice and handed them to Nate. "I'll use these to make table centerpieces."

"The awful artificial tree has to go." Nate motioned to a teen boy wearing a hoodie with a school name on it working the tree lot. "Let's buy a real one."

"A spectacular idea." Isabella hummed along with "O Christmas Tree."

Nate laughed. "No way am I singing in public, ever again."

"The public thanks you." She giggled.

Isabella accompanied Nate to roam in and out of the trees placed along the sidewalk.

The tree lot worker followed them.

"That's it." Isabella pointed to a smallish, perfectly shaped one. "That's the one I love."

"I love that one, too." Nate's was looking at Isabella, not the tree.

Her heart stuttered in confusion. She said nothing, pretending not to catch his obvious innuendo. *How does he expect me to react? How can I love a man who seems not to know the true meaning of family?* She couldn't fault him, she argued with herself. *He'd missed the closeness of a family while growing up. However, I know better than to believe you can change the one you love into becoming a different person.*

The teen grabbed through the branches onto the trunk of the tree. "Do you want this one?"

Nate dragged his gaze from Isabella to answer the boy. "We'll take it, and we'll need a stand."

She steadied her rattled self and left Nate to supervise the netting of the tree while she selected candles, ribbons, ornaments, and tinsel.

After the purchases, Nate shouldered the tree on their return walk to Fontana's.

Isabella managed the other packages, and she kept their banter light, pointedly ignoring their romantic moment.

Nate entered the shop with the tree and propped it against a wall.

Sal clapped. "Now, that's a tree."

Charlie echoed Sal's sentiments. "That's a tree, all right."

With a jerk of his thumb, Sal announced, "This old fake thing belongs in the alley's dumpster."

"Agree," Isabella exclaimed.

Together, the four dismantled the decorations from it.

Isabella held open the swinging kitchen door for Charlie and Sal to drag the fake tree to the alley door.

Beth moved out of the men's way. "Bella, we'll have another batch of cookies coming soon."

Angie pointed a spoon in Isabella's direction. "I hope we've got the glaze right this time."

"Thanks, both of you." Isabella sniffled tears back.

"I know Dottie sends us good vibes."

"I welcome good vibes." Angie shook the spoon toward a perceived heaven. "But, Dottie, can't you send down to us the secret to your glaze?"

Grinning, Isabella let the kitchen door swing shut and entered the bakery to see Nate wrestling the tree into the new stand. "Let me help you."

Nate shifted the tree to the side, and his gaze met hers. "Thanks."

Isabella's insides shifted all jittery. She took hold of the tree opposite him, relieved the branches hid her face. "On the count of three, we'll lift it."

"Good plan."

With a firm grip on the trunk, Isabella counted to three. Together, they raised it high and jammed its trunk into the stand's prongs.

"Let me check if it's straight." Isabella stepped from the tree and studied it for a moment. "Shift it to the right a smidge."

Nate obeyed.

"Oh, too much." Isabella used her hands to form a frame with the tree in the center. "Go a little to the left."

Again, Nate obeyed.

"That's it." Isabella grasped the trunk one more. "I'll hold it while you tighten the stand's bolts."

Nate's gaze once more found hers. He leaned to kiss her.

She ducked his attempt.

"I'll tighten the stand." He dropped to the floor and scootched under the tree, his long legs protruding out.

Isabella kept a firm grasp on the trunk, her fingers getting sticky from its sap. "Tell me when I can let go."

"Never."

"Excuse me?"

Nate rolled on his back and looked at Isabella. "Never let go."

Isabella felt the room tilt.

"Goodbye to the artificial tree," Charlie pronounced upon entering the room. "Hey. The tree's leaning to the right."

"No, you mean the left." Sal reached Isabella's side. "Let me hold it, and you look."

She stepped away, still shaky over Nate's romantic overtures. *Don't let his flirting rattle you, Isabella. He's Nate-the-Player, remember?* "You men figure this out. Don't forget to put some sugar water in the stand, too."

She cleaned the sticky sap from her fingers. Determined to keep her distance from Nate, Isabella busied herself with creating a centerpiece of evergreen boughs, candles, and red velvet ribbons for each table.

"Come on, Bella." Nate dangled an ornament toward her. "We need your help to string the lights and tinsel and hang the new ornaments."

Their clumsy attempt at trimming the tree reminded Isabella of the twins' tree decorating. She took the ornament from Nate, being careful to avoid letting their hands touch. "Yes, I think you could use my help."

The decorating went quickly with all involved.

Charlie helped Sal hang the star on the top.

Nate raised his arms as if signaling a touchdown. A ridiculously huge grin spread across his face. "I've gotta admit it. That's a pretty tree-mendous Christmas tree."

Isabella's throat closed up, preventing her from joining the laughter over Nate's pun. Her heart ached at how he looked like a kid in awe of everything Christmas. She bet his family never trimmed a tree together.

She surveyed the shop, and her breath caught at the sight. In a few, brief hours, they transformed "shabby" Fontana's into the cheery, welcoming bakery-bookshop café of her dreams. A sign propped inside the main bakery case labeled a space for Dottie's Cannoli Cookies. Trays of them for sale would make everything perfect.

I double dare shoppers to pass by Fontana's now without stopping.

Angie entered with plates of cookies in both hands and froze, her mouth agape.

Beth stepped from the kitchen and stopped at Angie's side. "Angie, what's wrong?" She took the plates from her.

"Oh, Isabella." Angie dab her tears with her apron. "The place looks so bright and cheery. I feel we've traveled back fifty years to our Christmas opening day."

Sal drew her into a hug. "Merry Christmas, Ang."

"Merry Christmas, Sal." Angie kissed him on the cheek.

Isabella held back her tears at the sight of them. She noticed Nate's eyes appeared watery, too. *This shop has so much life and love left in it. Damn you, Nate, for tearing it down.*

"Who wants a cannoli cookie?" Beth waved the plates.

Charlie plucked one off a plate. "What batch number does this make? You've kept us on a cannoli cookie sugar high all night."

"Honestly? I've lost track." Beth set the platters on a table and rolled her shoulders to relax them. "We are getting so close to Dottie's, but we're still off a bit."

Charlie finished another cookie. "They're delicious

to me." He checked his watch and shook his head. "It's the stroke of midnight." He pulled on his trench coat and scarf and gestured to the stack of flattened boxes, emptied of the books. "I'll toss these into the dumpster on my way."

"I'll help." Isabella followed him through the kitchen to prop open the back door. "Thank you so much, Charlie. For the books. And, for believing in me."

"You're welcome."

Despite his gruff voice, his eyes sparkled behind his spectacles. Isabella could tell he appreciated her thanks.

Where will you go after Fontana's closed? Now I'm sharing Sal and Angie's worry about you.

Chapter Fourteen

Isabella shut the kitchen's alley door and re-entered the cheery bakery, breathing in the intoxicating scents of the evergreen tree and the fresh-baked cookies.

Beth offered her a cookie. "The glaze isn't the same as your mom's, Bella. I'm getting discouraged."

Angie nodded. "We keep trying more and more orange zest."

Isabella nibbled at the cookie. "I see what you mean. Nate, what do you think?" She swirled to address him but found him gone. "Where has he gone?"

"Nate? He headed out." Sal slumped into a chair and stifled a yawn. "He's flying to New York City first thing in the morning."

Isabella pressed a hand against her stomach, which flip-flopped at the news. *He left without a goodbye. So typical of him. Why should I care? Yet, I do, darn it.* "He needs to get back to process the papers you've signed, I suppose." She struggled to keep her voice even.

"No." Sal looked at Angie. "We haven't signed them yet. It's a big decision."

"I've told you both and I'm telling you once more. Nate's right. You should sign. It's a substantial offer." Isabella again surprised herself with the words coming out of her mouth, but, sadly, she believed what she said.

"Yes." Sal's jutted out his chin. "We trust him and Diana. They're family. They wouldn't steer us in the wrong direction."

Isabella hoped neither Sal nor Angie noticed her cringe. *I fear Nate and Diana are sharks circling the Fontana's water, out for themselves.*

"Before I forget." Sal directed his comment toward Isabella. "Nate says he will see you at Jen's wedding. He asked for you to save him a cookie and a dance."

Beth gave Isabella's arm a pinch. "You didn't tell me you asked him to go."

"I didn't. And, ouch." Isabella rubbed her arm. "Sal, did Nate say who invited him?"

Sal opened his mouth to answer.

Angie shoved a cookie into it. "Isabella, I think saving Nate one of Dottie's delicious cookies will be a problem."

"Saving him a dance will be the bigger problem." Isabella clapped her hand over her mouth. "Did I say that out loud?"

"You did." Angie frowned. "But, we know you didn't mean it."

Yes I did.

Angie headed to the kitchen. "We'll try one more batch before calling it quits for the night."

"It's after midnight, Ang." Sal followed her. "Let it go until tomorrow."

"You can go to bed. I'm inspired to keep going." Angie put her hands on her hips. "What about it, girls?"

"It's already so late." Beth grinned. "I guess I can stay for one more batch. I'll text Owen."

"To the kitchen." Isabella charged toward the swinging door and propped it open. "Come on."

While Angie and Beth began preparing yet another batch of dough, Isabella stared at an orange on the counter. She tossed the fruit back and forth in her hands. "It's the orange taste in the glaze that's off. Agreed?"

"Yes." Beth paused stirring the cookie batter. "But, we haven't hit on the right measurement for the zest."

Angie nodded. "We've tried different amounts of almond and zest. We can't crack your mom's secret."

"Maybe we've misidentified an ingredient?" Isabella flung the orange high into the air and caught it. "Beth, you remember how my mom always kept freshly squeezed orange juice?"

"I do."

Angie scanned her copy of the recipe. "There's no mention of orange juice, Isabella. It says orange zest."

Isabella retrieved the original copy of the recipe from her handbag. She noticed a light line drawn through the word zest. "Oh, my instinct may be right. Look."

Angie and Beth peered over her shoulder to where she pointed.

"What if the wrinkle in the paper is a line drawn through the word zest? Could the ingredient for the glaze be juice from an orange? Not zest from an orange? Oranges. Sunshine."

"Let the sun," Angie said with a sing-song lilt.

Isabella joined her. "Shine in."

Angie hurried to a cabinet. "I'll get my juicer."

Isabella pressed the sliced oranges through the juicer. After measuring the amount for the glaze, she poured some of the fresh, delicious liquid into three glasses for each of them to drink while they waited for a new batch of cookies to finish baking.

They glazed the warm cookies.

Isabella claimed the first taste test. From the first bite, the perfect flavor burst forth in her mouth, transporting her back to childhood, enjoying a fresh-baked cannoli cookie snack on Christmas Eve with Mom and Dad, before setting out a plate of them for Santa. *We did, Mom. We let the sun shine in.* After devouring the cookie, she waved another in the air. "Ladies, we have channeled my mother. Here's to Dottie's Cannoli Cookies."

Beth and Angie tipped theirs against Isabella, in a toast.

"To Dottie." Angie's voice cracked with emotion.

"To Dottie," Beth squealed.

"To Dottie." Isabella's eyes teared.

Angie handed a napkin to Isabella. "I would love to sell these as our Christmas cookie special until we close. Will you allow me to feature them, Isabella?"

Isabella dabbed at her tears. "Allow you, Angie? I've already designated a space in the bakery case for them. But, remember, I'll need at least six dozen for Jen's cookie table."

Beth spoke through a bite of cookie. "Don't worry, Bella. Angie and I can manage. I've forgotten how much I love baking."

"Am I missing a party?" Sal entered the kitchen, dressed in his old-fashioned long nightgown with a cap on his head.

"You're rocking the pj's, Sal." Isabella's eyes widened.

Beth joined in Isabella's laughter

"Shush, you two." Angie placed a hand over her mouth but her eyes laughed.

Sal sniffed the air. "More cannoli cookies?"

"Not any cannoli cookies," Angie gave a triumphant shout, "Dottie's."

"Let me be the judge of that." After Sal devoured the last bite, he removed his nightcap and tossed it in the air. "Dottie, they've done you proud."

Isabella floated through the motions of helping Angie and Beth clean the kitchen. She thought about all the women of her family who baked these cookies. Her great-great-grandmother would be proud of her namesake. She basked in the beaming smiles of Sal, Angie, and Beth. *Enjoy this triumphant moment. We've saved Dottie's Cannoli Cookies for the world to enjoy…but we have to say goodbye to Fontana's. Again, damn you, Nate. Why can't I banish you from my mind…and heart?*

"Time for bed." Angie hugged each girl and retired to join Sal in their apartment upstairs.

"Time for us to get home." Beth yawned. "We can call a ride service if you're too sleepy to drive."

"I'm wide awake, running on cannoli cookie energy." Isabella swung into her coat, giving her half-snort laugh. "I have enough sugar in me to power through until the end of next year." She pulled from the pockets her hat and one glove. *Why can't I keep track of these dang things? Did I drop it on the way back from the Christmas tree lot? I remember taking them off right before we arrived back at the bakery.*

Isabella's stomach contracted into a tight ball. She'd lost a glove before, and Nate returned it. That had been the day she first learned about his real purpose for being at Fontana's. *How dare you disappear again, without a word? How dare you ask for me to save you a cookie and a dance at the wedding reception?* She gritted her teeth. *Damn you, Nate.*

Chapter Fifteen

Isabella drove Beth and the twins the next day to the shop, planning to be the first customers into the brightened-up and Christmas cheery Fontana's Corner Bakery.

"Look at that." Beth gestured to the crunch of people filling the bakery. "We won't be the first after all."

"Wow. I guess the new look and signage snags people's attention. The bakery is swamped with customers. Sal and Angie will need our help." Isabella flew toward the bakery.

"Coming." Beth helped the girls from the backseat and scurried with them into Fontana's. "I'll call Owen to get Hazel and Rachel."

"That's a good idea. Angie's going to need you to crank out more cannoli cookies." Isabella pointed to the few remaining in the bakery case. "They're a hit."

Sal waved over the crowd at the bakery cases. "Am I glad to see you."

Beth disappeared into the kitchen with the girls.

Isabella grabbed an apron from the hook by the cash register. She roamed the shop, manning the book nooks and answering questions about the bakery items. If customers agreed and signed a release, she photographed them and filmed their testimonials about Fontana's for a Happy Retirement video for Angie and Sal.

Charlie entered at his usual late afternoon time. He

found Isabella at the register. "Busy day?"

Isabella finished ringing a customer's sale before answering. "Hi, Charlie. Join the crowd. We're super-busy." She motioned for the next customer.

Charlie joined her behind the counter. "Got another apron?"

"I do." Isabella handed it to him.

He tied it on. "I got this. You go do whatever else needs your attention."

"You're a god-send, Charlie." Isabella snapped a photo of him and left him in charge of the register. She pushed through the swinging door into the kitchen to check on Angie and Beth. She found two exhausted bakers sitting on stools at the work table and two trays of cannoli cookies needing glazing.

Beth stared at the bowl. "I don't think I can mix one more bowl of dough."

The pastry brush fell from Angie's grasp. "Or glaze one more cookie."

"Let me." Isabella grabbed the pastry brush and glazed the warm cookies. "I'm relieving you two of duty. We're closing early. We'll wait on the customers in the store now, but no more."

With a sigh, Beth rested her head on the counter.

Angie nodded. "Thanks."

Isabella hustled into the bakery with the two trays of the cookies. "Here you go, Sal. The last ones for the day."

He slid the trays into the place designated Dottie's Cannoli Cookies. He placed a few on the sample platter on the bakery case and broke them apart into bite-sized pieces. "Once customers try a bite, they're hooked. Dottie would be so proud."

"She sure would be." Isabella pulled in a deep breath. *Mom, I'm making you famous.*

"The books are flying out of here, too." Sal pointed to the book nooks. "Wherever you and Beth open your bakery-bookstore café, it will be a hit."

"I think so, too." Isabella patted Sal's shoulder. "It's been a day, huh?"

"Passable." With an impish grin, Sal waited on the next customer.

You old codger. You don't fool me. You're thrilled. Isabella flipped the open sign on the door to closed. She played traffic controller to ensure all customers were waited upon, checked out, and ushered from the shop with her personal invitation for them to return.

After the last customer departed, Sal pulled off his apron and collapsed into the first chair he came to. He called to Charlie, "I thought my eyes were playing tricks, seeing you at the register. What in the world?"

"It's not rocket science to run a register," Charlie grumbled. He removed his apron and joined Sal. "You owe me coffee and cookies, you know. I didn't get to read a single page of my new mystery, either."

Beth came through the kitchen door, massaging her shoulders and groaning.

Angie followed and rushed to hug Isabella. "What a day."

Sal laughed. "Isabella's given the old place a new spirit and our old selves renewed energy, hasn't she Ang?"

"I'll say. It'll be harder than ever to say goodbye, but we'll say it with our heads lifted high."

Isabella blinked to keep her tears in check. She motioned to Beth and Charlie. "These two get credit, too."

Angie wrapped her arm around Beth's waist. "This gal's some baker."

Beth elbowed Angie. "I'm learning from the best."

Charlie harrumphed. "It's getting a little thick in here, don't you think?"

Isabella sat next to him and laughed. "You're an unconvincing old grump, Charlie."

Angie and Beth joined them at the table.

Sal glanced around him and swept his arm in the air. "I wish Nate were here to see this." He shook his head in disbelief. "Isabella, you and Beth have transformed Fontana's into a new place within its old walls. If only you girls could keep it going."

Isabella bowed her head. *If only.*

****

With two days remaining before Christmas Eve, Isabella tweaked Fontana's website to spotlight Dottie's Cannoli Cookies and include some of the video testimonials from customers. She showed Angie and Sal.

They agreed she could let it go live.

Online orders flooded in for Dottie's cookies, books, and bakery gift baskets. By Christmas Eve, Isabella welcomed a break in the madness. At least she'd been too busy to mope over Nate.

Sal and Angie hosted a Christmas Eve luncheon and toasted the week's success before shooing everyone out with shouts of Merry Christmas and hugs.

Isabella leaned back behind the wheel and gave an exhausted sigh. She watched Beth and Charlie cross the intersection to add a donation into Santa's charity bucket. Worry nudged at her about Charlie being alone on Christmas Day. He didn't accept their invitation to come to Beth's for Christmas dinner. *I know how it feels to be alone, Charlie. I'll think of you.*

She stared at the *Closed for Christmas* sign dangling from Fontana's door. In a week the closed sign would be permanent. Soon, a parking deck would replace the bakery. The one thing cushioning the bitterness for Isabella was knowing she and Beth would open their place in the coming year. Staring into the bakery's Christmas-painted store windows, she let herself conjure memories of it in years past. She could almost see herself as a little girl, sitting with her parents, Sal, and Angie at the corner table.

The passenger door opened and a whoosh of cold air jarred Isabella from the past.

"Donation made." Beth settled in for the drive home. "We survived, Bella. We'll have an entire holiday weekend to recuperate. I can't say I'll miss baking cannoli cookies for a few days."

"I bet Angie feels the same way." Isabella reversed from the parking space and began the drive to Beth's. "It's strange, you know." She forced her words through a lump forming in her throat. "I've been channeling Dad through Charlie's books and Mom through the cannoli cookies."

"It's been quite the spectacular few days, Bella." Beth patted her arm. "At least we have a few more days next week before Fontana's doors shut forever."

Isabella nodded. Her thoughts shifted to Nate. *What have you been doing since you disappeared...again? Have you been celebrating early over the success of your parking conglomerate deal? Sal and Angie haven't signed yet, but I know they will. Too bad you weren't a believer, Nate Elliot. Based on our success these past days, it's obvious we could've kept Fontana's Corner Bakery open for five more decades.*

****

Isabella awakened Christmas morning to the excited screams of the twins. She stretched her body long in the bed and exhaled a sigh of contentment. Being with Beth and her family emphasized how alone she'd been in Miami.

Memories of Christmas mornings with her parents tweaked her heart. *You both must be so glad I'm no longer isolating myself from where I truly belong.* Her imagination wanders to Nate celebrating Christmas with his date for the wedding. She blinked back tears. *For the umpteenth time, Nate is not the right man for me.*

Thinking of him reminded her of the inevitable. In a few days Fontana's Corner Bakery would close forever. Isabella curled her toes, dreading the reality. At least it would close on a high note of success, sending Sal and Angie into a proud, well-deserved retirement.

The twins' banging against Isabella's bedroom door roused her from her recollections. Before she could ask them to enter, they burst in. The Christmas morning madness descended.

"It's snowing," the girls screamed in synch.

"Get up, Aunt Bella." Rachel bounced onto one side of the bed.

Hazel bounced onto the other side. "Santa's come." She placed a finger on the side of her nose and grinned at Rachel.

Rachel returned the signal.

Isabella realized what it meant. *Dang it. They have been playing along with believing. But, shouldn't everyone? It's part of the spirit of the holiday.* "Let me up. You're smothering me." She sprang out of bed, sending both girls flying off, and threw on her robe. "Time to open presents."

Isabella raced the twins to the den.

Owen and Beth sat on the sofa, each sipping large Christmas mugs of coffee.

Beth offered Isabella one. "Start imbibing the caffeine now. The day will be long and hectic."

Isabella sipped the coffee and watched the twins tear into their Santa gifts and the gifts she gave them. Their earsplitting screeches confirmed how much they loved the doll clothes, matching nightgowns, accessories, and books.

When the twins' excitement wound down, Isabella handed Beth a small wrapped box. "Here's a little something for you."

"And, I have one more something for you." Beth gave Isabella a flat, large box. "Let's open at the same time?"

"Go." Isabella tore into her package, keeping her eyes on Beth.

"Oh my." Beth pulled out a silver chain with three tiny silver charms of a spatula, a mixer, and a spoon dangling from it.

"For Beth-the-baker." Isabella grinned.

"It's adorably perfect." Beth fastened it on. "Now, look at yours."

Isabella pulled from the gift box the rendering of their bakery-bookstore, matted and framed. "Oh, Beth. I thought I'd lost this drawing."

"Remember you put it on the refrigerator? I took a photo to print and frame. Is the original lost?"

"Yes. I put it in my business plan folder I've

somehow misplaced, so I am so glad you snapped a picture. Thanks so much."

"You're welcome, partner." Beth held her hand out.

Isabella shook with her. "Merry Christmas, partner."

****

With the storm of the gift-giving subsided, Isabella sat at the kitchen table with another cup of coffee and a pastry from Fontana's, listening to Beth and Owen playing with the girls in the den. The ping on her phone surprised her.

—*Merry Christmas*—

When she recognized the sender, her heart rammed into her throat. Nate the Player. Hesitating over what to text back, Isabella finally decided on a Christmas tree emoji with no accompanying words. Her phone did not ping again, and Isabella's mood shifted to indignation. *No way am I going to let you ruin my day by checking every minute for a message.*

Isabella took the stairs two at a time and entered her room. She swiped off her phone and tossed it on her bed. *Time for a shower. I'll wash you, Nate Elliot, right out of my hair.*

****

For the rest of the Christmas day, Isabella reveled in holiday cheer of snow angels, hot chocolate, games, and a huge dinner with all the trimmings topped with pumpkin pie. The twins demanded to watch the movie *Elf* before crashing into bed. Isabella took charge of the girls' bedtime preparation and snapped photos of them with their dolls, dressed in her gift of matching nightgowns.

Over a nightcap of Irish coffee, Isabella relaxed

under a Christmas throw on one end of the den's couch facing Beth, nestled under another throw at the other end. Owen snored from the recliner by the fireplace. The fire's dancing flames and the Christmas tree lights cast a warm glow throughout the room. *It's A Wonderful Life* flickered on the television, muted.

Isabella tapped a foot against Beth's. "Thanks for including me in your Christmas. And for letting me crash here until I find a place."

"Our pleasure." Beth air-toasted with her mug.

Isabella lifted hers for the air-click.

"I can't believe the wedding is almost here." Beth lifted one eyebrow. "Are you going to save you-know-who a cookie and a dance?"

Isabella gaped at her friend. "While his date shoots poisonous darts in my direction? No thanks."

"Who could be his date?" Beth's tone resonated with curiosity. She traced the rim of her mug with her finger. "I know how to find out. We can ask to see the RSVP list."

"I'm not wasting Jen's time on Nate." Isabella poked her foot against Beth's again, this time harder. "Or my time, either."

"I disagree. I still like him."

For a second time in the day, Isabella's heart rammed into her throat. *Why can't my desire for that man evaporate?* She closed her eyes, but Nate materialized behind her lids. *How right your lips feel upon mine. We connect over life's losses and their heart's needs. But I expect more from you than you can give. Closing the deal will award you the success you crave, even if it means treading on other's hearts including Sal's, Angie's...and mine.*

Not wanting disappointment to ruin the day, Isabella changed the subject. "I'm even more convinced our bakery-bookshop café will be a success. These past few days has shown our plan will work. We'll scout out another location in this neighborhood. With Simon's help, we'll find backers. He calls them angel investors."

"Angels. How nice. Who doesn't need an angel to invest in their dreams?" Beth rested her head back into the crook of the sofa. "It has been fun. The sugar high has been real, too." She yawned. "I think I've been baking Dottie's Cannoli Cookies in my sleep."

Isabella laughed. "Better than in my nightmares, where I would be burning them." She wriggled her body to sit straighter. Her hand touched her book locket. "Seriously, Beth. The cookies are a hit, and the sales have been through the roof. We're on to something."

As if mirroring Isabella, Beth's hand traveled to her baker's necklace. "I agree, Partner. We're going to do this."

"Is your heart thumping as hard as mine?"

"Harder. Should I wake Owen up? In case we need CPR?"

"Nah, let the doctor sleep. He'll need to resuscitate us on our café's opening day."

Isabella swung her body to a seated position. "Nora Roberts calls me. I'm halfway through the book." She tipped her mug to Beth for one last toast of the night. "Cheers. Merry Christmas to all, and to all a good night."

Chapter Sixteen

The Monday after Christmas Isabella reported with Beth to Fontana's for its last days of business before its door shuttered. The shop, so shabby and empty of customers when she first visited upon her return home, now throbbed with energetic shoppers.

The flow of customers that began the week before Christmas continued, both in-person and online. Angie and Beth began baking Dottie's Cannoli Cookies early in the morning, and by end of each business day, none remained.

The used books Charlie donated dwindled until one stack remained, proving to Isabella a market existed for trade ins and low-priced purchases by avid readers. The books themselves produced little profit, but they attracted customers who enjoyed lingering over purchasing multiple coffees and cookies.

Isabella labeled some tables 'book nook' ones, where strangers sat together to discuss authors. It sparked another idea in Isabella's business mind. *Beth and I will offer book clubs at our place. We can invite authors and host signings.*

As if in a blink, the last day arrived. Isabella fought to control her tears every time she glimpsed the sign announcing Closing Day. Charlie's entrance caught Isabella by surprise, for he always arrived later in the day. *How could time have swept by so quickly?* With a glance at the clock, the sadness she'd fought all day to resist overwhelmed her. Soon the bakery's doors would close forever.

Charlie jerked his thumb toward the sign. "Guess it's the end of an era, Sal."

"Afraid so, Charlie." Sal rested his elbows on top of the bakery case, his usual stance when conversing with customers. "It's been a quick fifty years, pal." He wiped away sentimental tears with his handkerchief.

Isabella averted her gaze, not wanting either old man to see her welling tears.

"I got something for you." Sal held a photo in his hands. "Angie began taking pictures of our customers on our opening day. She used one of those cameras that shot out a picture to develop before your eyes. It was newfangled for the time. Through the years, we covered the walls with so many merry faces. I've been giving the photos to customers." He handed Charlie his picture. "Here you go, old friend. Remember our opening day at Christmas time so many years ago? You came in with your book asking for a cup of coffee, cookies, and a quiet place to end your day."

Isabella fought to hold back her tears at the sight of the two old men reminiscing. She'd asked Sal to let her family's picture remain on the wall until the end of the day. Once the moment would finally come when he would hand it to her, she knew she'd bawl enough tears to float Noah's ark.

"Did you sign those papers, yet?" Charlie asked, staring at the photograph. "The parking deck offer?"

"Ah, not yet. Nate asked us to hold off until tomorrow. He might've found another buyer."

"What do you mean, Sal?" Goosebumps raced over

Isabella. "Is there a chance someone other than the parking conglomerate will buy you out? When did you find this out?"

"Nate mentioned something along those lines that night we redecorated the place, before he asked me to tell you he'd see you at the wedding." Sal busied himself with preparing another pot of coffee.

"Who did you say he's taking to the wedding?" Isabella projected a nonchalance she didn't feel.

"Oh, he's taking a gal named Nina. We've met her a few times."

The flight attendant? Nate acted as though nothing existed between them. What a liar.

Angie pushed through the kitchen swinging door, holding a stack of to go boxes. "Sal, these are all orders for the Jen's cookie table." She scowled at him. "And, keep your mouth shut, why don't you?"

Isabella switched her focus off Nate and Nina to the possibility of another offer. "Sal, think hard. What exactly did Nate tell you about another offer?"

Angie frowned. "Are you keeping something from me, Sal?"

"Why do I open my trap?" Sal placed his full attention on Charlie. "Do you want your regular order of cannoli cookies and coffee?"

"Don't you change the subject on me, Sal Fontana." Angie clapped her hand on his shoulder. "Spit it out, right this instance."

"Uh." Sal fiddled with his apron. "Well, Nate didn't share any specifics. He mentioned another offer could come, but he said nothing more. It could be another parking deck deal, for all I know."

Or it could be a deal that could keep Fontana's

open. Isabella exhaled a sigh of irritation. *Why didn't Sal ask for more information?*

"I think I'll go sit." Charlie stuck his snapshot into his paperback and sat in his normal spot. He slid out of his trench coat and draped it over the back of the chair.

Isabella checked out Charlie's bowtie now on full view. Noticing his neckwear each time he came into the bakery provided her a touchstone of comfort. Today's pattern was a red-nosed reindeer. It reminded her of how Nate and she sang with such abandon while doing kitchen duty. *Damn you, Nate.*

"Isabella, take Charlie his coffee and cookies, please?" Angie placed cookies on a dish before brushing back through the doors into the kitchen.

"Happy to, Angie." Isabella poured a cup of the newly brewed coffee and served it and the cookies to the old man. "Here you go." She joined him. "I'd love to see your photo."

"It's in here." He gave her his paperback.

She flipped the pages and found it. "What a keepsake." Isabella grinned. *Even the young adult Charlie sported a goatee, round spectacles, and bowtie.*

Charlie stared at her, his eyes behind his round spectacles appearing leaky. "You've updated this old place, Isabella." His voice sounded thick. "Too bad you couldn't have taken it over. Do you think you could have kept it going?"

The door chime rang, announcing a group of customers.

Isabella jumped up. "I've got to get back." She slid the photo back into the paperback before placing it on the table. "The answer to your question? Yes, I could have kept it going. In fact, Beth and I together would've run the hell out of this place, Charlie."

She hurried to the bakery cases, trying to keep her hopes dampened at Sal's news about Nate. Could his Merry Christmas text have meant he had news to share, but she'd blown him off? *Don't be silly. His Merry Christmas meant nothing. For all I know, he could have included me in a group text he sent to many. The name I entered him as in my phone says it all. He is Nate the player.*

The rest of the day, Isabella refused to think about Nate finding an offer to keep the bakery open or his bringing Nina to the wedding.

At closing time, Charlie remained.

Isabella, along with the exhausted Beth, Angie, and Sal, joined him at his table.

"I guess I'll load the boxes of Dottie's Cannoli Cookies for the wedding reception into my car." Isabella stretched her legs out to the side of her chair. "But first, I need my aching feet to quit barking at me."

Beth checked her phone and stood. "Isabella, are you ready to head home? A frantic Owen has sent several texts begging for my help to get the twins ready for the wedding rehearsal tonight."

"Hold on a minute, Beth. Here's your photo." Sal placed it in her hand, his voice choking. "Thanks for everything these past days and past years." He pointed to the wall behind the cash register counter. "Isabella, you need to get yours."

Isabella did not react, wanting to postpone the inevitable.

"Was I ever this young?" Beth stared at her snapshot. "If anyone cries, it'll be the end of me. Remember, there's no crying in baking."

Angie grabbed Beth's hand. "You're one heck of a baker. I hope you and Isabella will open your place, soon."

The rap on the store's glass door drew everyone's attention. Beth traipsed toward it. "I'll tell them we're closed."

Isabella hated the finality of those words. She glimpsed a delivery truck at the curb. "Are you expecting a package, Sal?"

"Nope."

Angie placed both hands on either side of her head. "I can't handle one more thing to pack. I'm already overwhelmed."

Beth opened the door.

The delivery guy motioned with the device for signing.

"You'll need to sign, Sal." Beth stepped away.

After signing, Sal brought a flat envelope to the table.

Beth followed, glimpsing at it over Sal's shoulder. "It's from Simon's office."

"What?" Isabella's eyebrows arched. "What business does Simon handle for you, Sal?"

"None I know about." Sal unzipped the envelope's tab.

"Hurry, Sal." Angie lifted prayer hands high. "I hope it's not awful news."

Sal read over the enclosed document to himself before handing it to Isabella. She read it aloud:

Dear Mr. and Mrs. Fontana,

We represent an angel investor who wishes to purchase Fontana's Corner Bakery. It will remain a neighborhood bakery under the management of employees the investor hires. Please visit the bank at 1:00 pm tomorrow. The purchase price will meet your offer currently under review.

Sal reclaimed the letter from Isabella. "An angel investor?"

"Who could it be?" Angie asked.

Charlie adjusted his spectacles. "Any ideas, Sal?"

"Zero."

Beth took the letter from Sal and read it over. "Did Simon mention a competing, interested buyer to you, Isabella?"

"He did not." Isabella shook her head.

"Who do you suppose the buyer will choose to manage the shop?" Angie clasped her hands. "We'd love to suggest you girls."

"We'd accept in a flash, but our angel, as we shall call him or her, might have people in mind." Isabella glanced once more at the offer before giving it back to Sal.

He inserted the letter into the envelope. "Could you come with me to this meeting, Isabella? You too, Beth."

"We can't, Sal. We're busy with the wedding all day tomorrow." Isabella cast a hopeful glance toward Beth. "Unless we could slip away for a bit?"

Beth shook her head. "You know how wedding days are all-consuming. But, we can ask Simon at the rehearsal tonight if he knows anything." She checked the time on her phone. "Let's get moving, Bella."

Sal fished his phone from his apron pocket. "I'll call Nate. Maybe he knows about this angel."

Worry chased away Isabella's excitement. *What if Nate knows nothing about this offer? What if our angel and the parking lot conglomerate get into a bidding war?*

Would Angel's pockets be deep enough to win?

Beth shook Isabella's coat at her. "We must leave. Now."

"Okay, okay." Isabella slipped into her outerwear and grabbed her handbag from under the register's counter. "Keep me posted, Sal and Angie. We'll also let you know what Simon says."

"Don't forget the cookies for the reception." Charlie pointed at the boxes on the bakery counter.

Isabella grabbed them and flashed Charlie a smile. "Thanks. What would the cookie table be without them? Sal, any answer from Nate?"

"Not yet." Sal tapped on his phone. "I'm messaging him, asking him to call me right away."

Angie shrugged. "He could be on the flight back from New York, and his phone is off?"

A picture of Nate and Nina together flashed into Isabella's imagination. *They make a striking couple. At least I don't have to encounter them at the rehearsal, but I will have to see them at the wedding. Great.* She followed Beth out of Fontana's, her spirits buoyed over Fontana's being saved. *Unless Nate messes with our angel.*

Chapter Seventeen

At the rehearsal, Isabella and Beth cornered Simon.

He claimed no knowledge of a last-minute angel investor buying out Fontana's. After placing a few calls, he informed them of the legitimacy of the offer. "An angel has come from upon high. Fontana's on the Corner is saved, if all goes as planned," Simon concluded.

The news gave Isabella something more than the impending wedding to celebrate at the rehearsal dinner. When she collapsed into bed after the long evening, she envied whomever the angel hired to run the place. *No matter who you hire, I'll help the new management keep Fontana's a success.*

****

At nine o'clock the next morning, Isabella and Beth joined the wedding party at the hair salon for hair, makeup and nails. Over mimosas and snacks, the twists and turns of the conversation led to Nate and Nina.

"I didn't invite either of them," Jen declared. "I delegated the responsibility of RSVP and table seating to our mom's. Simon and I couldn't handle the drama. Do you have any idea how many relatives don't speak to each other?"

The day progressed to their arrival at the church to get dressed in the bride's room. Isabella tried to ignore the knot in her stomach over her phone calls and texts to Sal going unanswered. Not even glimpsing her book locket shining against the satin green bodice of the bridesmaid dress eased her sense of foreboding. *Has our angel withdrawn the offer and flown away? Will Nate's client win, after all?*

Isabella's apprehension over Sal and Angie's meeting at the bank supplanted her dread over seeing Nate with Nina. She moved through the motions of the pre-wedding photographs in a preoccupied daze. The wedding photographer kept reminding her of where to stand and when to smile.

Before they moved into positions for the processional, Beth took her aside. "I hate to scold you, but you've let worrying about the fate of Fontana's and seeing Nate distract you. You're a bridesmaid, and Jen needs you to celebrate her big day."

Isabella inhaled a deep breath. *I'll have to accept whatever has happened, so why let it ruin the night?* "You're right. I need to pull myself together. Thanks for being so honest with me."

"That-a-girl." Beth slapped her on the back.

"Hey." Isabella adjusted the gown's bodice. "Don't mess up the dress." She plucked her cell phone from the handy pocket. "Where's Kate and Anna and their little guys? Ethan and EJ are adorable in their tuxes, and Rachel and Hazel are gorgeous. Let's get a group picture of them together."

When the processional commenced, Isabella passed Sal and Angie, who sat at the end of the first aisle.

They both motioned thumbs up.

Isabella beamed a smile. *Fontana's was saved.* She almost floated to the altar. When she faced the huge gathering of attendees and caught sight of Nate and Nina, the lightness in her limbs turned heavy.

The two sat with their heads together, whispering. They appeared comfortable together, as if they'd been a couple for some time.

The music's crescendo announced the bride's entrance, and everyone stood, blocking Nate and Nina from her view. Isabella breathed a silent thanks. She swiveled to the front of the church and tightened her hold on her bridesmaid bouquet, fighting the seesawing of her emotions over Nate. *Thank you, Jen and Simon, for choosing the Rites of Marriage and not a full mass and communion. I would have collapsed.*

Isabella kept her eyes downcast during the recessional to avoid Nate and Nina. The after-ceremony pictures helped distract her until the photographer directed everyone except the married couple to the reception tent. *I won't be able to avoid Nate for much longer.*

She located her place at the long bridal table and placed her bouquet at her seat before threading her way through the reception throng to view the cookie table. Her insides danced at its untouched glory. It offered every cookie variety imaginable. *Look, Mom. There's Dottie's Cannoli Cookies, piled high on several multi-tiered circular serving dishes. You're center stage, as usual.*

"A glass of champagne?"

"Yes, thanks." Isabella turned to accept the offer, but her hand fell limply to her side.

Nate stood before her managing the stems of two flutes of champagne in one hand and her missing winter glove in the other. His blue tie accented the blueness of his eyes…eyes in which she could get lost, if she allowed herself. He did not seem subdued, as she would have expected over his loss of the Fontana deal.

He held out the glove. "You dropped this the night we picked out the Christmas tree for Fontana's."

She snatched it. "You mean the night you disappeared. Again."

"Uh, yes. I have a long explanation to share. Again." He held out a glass. "First, let's toast to the bride and groom and to the legendary Dottie's Cannoli Cookies. They'll be the hit of the cookie table. I have no doubt."

"I have no doubt you and your date will enjoy them." Isabella took a fortifying sip of champagne. "Don't you need to get back to Nina?"

"She won't miss me. Her husband has arrived." Nate lifted his glass in Nina's direction. She and a smallish, balding man lifted their glasses in return. "Nina and I are step-siblings from Diana's marriage number three."

"B-but," Isabella stammered in surprise. "You told me you have no siblings."

"Semantics. I stay in touch with Nina, but none of the others. Simon and her husband Chris work together. Simon was scheduled to attend an end-of-year conference, but his return would be today, an obvious conflict with the wedding. He asked Chris to attend, meaning he'd miss the wedding."

Isabella remembered Simon's phone call at their appointment. He had been talking to Chris.

"Nina asked me to escort her to the wedding. Chris surprised us by making it back in time. It seems I'm the one now without a date."

"I see." Isabella offered him her glove. "Perhaps you could pocket this and escort me the rest of the evening."

He swirled the glove into the air while bowing. "At your service, m'lady."

Chapter Eighteen

The band sounded a fanfare before Isabella could prompt Nate to explain his absence.

"Ladies and Gentlemen, I present the newlyweds. Jen and Simon, Mr. and Mrs. Johnson."

Isabella and Nate set their glasses on the cookie table and joined the clapping, which faded as the couple entered the dance floor for their first dance. The father-daughter and mother-son dances followed.

Isabella's hand touched the book locket, and her chest felt hollow, yet heavy at the same time. *Mom, you'll not be part of my wedding, whenever the day may come. Dad, you'll not be there to walk me down the aisle and have the first dance.*

"I need a little air," she whispered to Nate. She hurried to one of the tent's exits and stepped out into snow swirling about her. The cold air cut through her thin bridesmaid dress.

Nate appeared by her side. Without a word, he draped his suit jacket about her shoulders and drew her close. "I'm sorry."

She kept her face averted. "About what?"

"All this must make you think about your wedding and who you'll be missing."

"Yes." Isabella snuggled his jacket closer about her, touched at how he understood without her explaining. His cologne clung to it, and she breathed in the scent she'd come to associate with him.

Nate whispered in her ear, "I'm also sorry I left without speaking with you. Again."

She sidestepped from standing too close.

"Remember the day at Fontana's when Uncle Sal and Charlie discussed the sale of the store? You rushed away and left your folder on the table. I studied its contents and could see the potential in your business plan. I should've given you the opportunity to explain fully your idea that night at Beth's."

"Thanks, but it doesn't matter, though. You were right. I couldn't raise the money to compete with your client's offer. Besides—"

Nate interrupted. "I should have listened to you and offered to help—"

"Shh." Isabella placed a finger on his lips. "I have to know, though. Sal said you told him to hold off on signing the parking deck deal. You were working on another one? He attempted to contact you about the surprise offer from the angel investor."

A brainstorm struck her. *You don't seem upset at all over the loss of your parking lot deal. Could you be acting so upbeat because you represent our angel?* She lifted an eyebrow, in a knowing manner. "What can you tell me about this angel investor?"

Nate removing her finger from his lips and squeezed her hand tightly. "Before we discuss the angelic bolt from out of the blue, let's talk about your business plan. I saw its potential, so I snapped photos and emailed them to my mother."

"You sent my plan to your mother?" Isabella's voice held surprise at the mention of Diana. "You told me you two barely speak."

"True. But because of you, I wanted to change that."

"Because of me?"

"Yes. You showed me how family should care for each other, not use each other." Nate took her other hand and squeezed both. "I flew back to New York to ask Diana to buy out Fontana's. She could secure Sal and Angie's retirement and reunite our family. You and Beth could manage the bakery until you purchased it from Diana." He let go of her and stepped back, shaking his head. "It was a grand scheme."

"Oh, Nate." Isabella placed her hands on his shoulders, her heart skipping a beat from happiness. *You are a good guy, after all.* "Do Sal and Angie realize our angel is Diana?"

Nate let out a peal of laughter.

Isabella frowned, confused. "What's so funny?"

"I said it *was* a grand scheme." Nate ran a hand through his hair, his brilliant blue eyes dulled. "Diana flat rejected me. She has no maternal bones, remember? In fact, she threatened to fire me if I didn't return to close the parking conglomerate deal. Sal's phone call telling us about the buyer meant my deal was kaput, so…"

"Nate. Your mother fired you? You must be devastated."

"Yes, she fired me, but no, I'm not devastated." Happiness returned to his eyes. He grabbed her hands again and brought them against his chest.

She felt his heart pounding.

He cocked an eyebrow. "I'm thrilled an investor materialized out of thin air. Uncle Sal and Aunt Angie signed the offer this afternoon. Have they told you the best part?"

"The best part?" Isabella echoed in a small voice.

"Sal and Angie recommended you and Beth to manage the bakery, and the investor's representative approved."

The thrumming of a thousand butterflies exploded within Isabella. "I can't believe it."

"It gets better. The deal required a change to the bakery's name."

"It won't be Fontana's anymore?"

"No. It's now Dottie's Corner Café."

"Dottie's?" Isabella whispered. *Mom and Dad, you'll be part of it all*. Concern for Nate's future intruded on her joy. She stroked his cheek. "But, what about you? What will you do? Why do you seem happy?"

"Because I am. Diana feels a tad of maternal remorse. She gave me a reference for a commercial real estate company here, and I start with them next week. My parking lot conglomerate client remains with me. I've presented another location near the bakery, and they're very interested in purchasing it."

Isabella grinned. "I know the exact location."

Nate moved her hands to his lips and kissed her palms. "A move to Pittsburgh will be exactly what I need. I hear it's a pretty great place to live."

"Now that we both will be here." Isabella stood on her tiptoes and found his mouth with hers. She held her lips against his until her breath left her. "Let's find Beth and tell her the news," she whispered.

"Yes, I agree. I'm freezing."

"Here you go." Isabella slipped out of his jacket. "I don't need it any longer. Your kisses warmed me."

Hand-in-hand, she walked with him into the reception tent.

"Bella." Beth came their way, a huge smile creasing

her face. "I've been searching for you. It's time for the New Year countdown." She handed Isabella a New Year's party hat and horn.

"Let me." Nate adjusted the hat on Isabella's head.

"We have a lot to celebrate in this new year." Isabella blew the horn in Beth's ear.

Beth ducked, laughing. "I've heard. Dottie's Corner Café."

"Our bakery-bookshop dream, come true." Isabella grabbed Beth into a hug.

Beth whispered, "What's happening with Nate?"

"Everything fantastic, and more," Isabella whispered back. She saw Charlie, dapper in a black suit and solid red bowtie. "Do you think Sal and Angie updated Charlie? Fontana's has meant so much to him."

"I think Charlie must know." Nate grabbed a party hat from a passing server and put it on. "He's looking pretty happy at the cookie table. By the way, did you ever find your folder with your business plan in it? I could have sworn I asked Charlie to return it to you."

"Did you?" Isabella's brain revved into overdrive. Charlie hadn't given her the folder, so what happened to it? When she'd flipped through Charlie's tattered paperback to find the snapshot of him, she'd seen on the inside cover the name C. Richard Fallon. She assumed the previous owner wrote it. *Am I on the edge of solving not only the lost folder mystery, but another more important one?*

Isabella fetched her phone from her pocket and searched on the name C. Richard Fallon. Scrolling, she found no images, but the search results presented articles about a reclusive rare book collector by the same name. The sales of first editions by this collector amounted to upward of millions of dollars. The first time she'd seen Charlie, Sal mentioned he lived a hermit-like life…and he collected books. They'd never shared his surname, and she'd never asked. *What if Charlie collected first editions? What if Charlie and C. Richard Fallon were one and the same?*

Isabella tapped Nate's arm. "I'll be right back." She made her way to Charlie. "Hello, you cookie thief. Don't you know the cookie table rule? No cookies until after toasts and dinner."

"I won't be staying much longer." Charlie took another cannoli cookie. "It's past my bedtime already."

"I guess I'll join you in breaking the rules." Isabella took one from the tray. "Did you hear? I'll be running Dottie's Corner Café. The bakery-bookshop will be a dream come true."

"Excellent news." He took another bite of cookie. "I predict these will be your top seller."

"I am betting on them to be." Isabella pointed her cookie at him. "I've been meaning to ask you. Nate said he asked you to return my business plan folder I left on the table the day Sal told you about the parking deck offer."

Charlie tugged on his red bowtie. "I don't remember him asking."

"Oh. It seems I have a mystery on my hands." Isabella took a small nibble of her cookie. "Do you think Mr. Fallon can help me?"

"Mr. Fallon enjoys an intriguing mystery." Charlie walked a few steps away from Isabella before turning back, eyes gleaming behind his spectacles. "I understand he's partial to small corner bakeries, too. He's planning to sell to a fine young lady one day in the near future."

He tapped his finger to the side of his nose.

"Charlie, you sly old angel." Isabella returned the signal. *Your secret remains safe with me.*

"May I have a cookie?" Nate snatched hers from Isabella's hand.

A roving photographer snapped their photo.

"I'll have to get a copy for Dottie's photo wall." Isabella tucked her arm under Nate's. "I'll hang it next to the one of my family. I never took it down."

The band leader called out "Countdown to midnight."

Isabella and Nate roared along with the crowd.

TEN
NINE
EIGHT
SEVEN
SIX
FIVE
FOUR
THREE
TWO
ONE

At the stroke of midnight, Nate swept Isabella into his arms for a New Year kiss amidst the cheers and strands of Auld Lang Syne. "Happy New Year, Bella. I hope I'll be the one who always returns your lost gloves. Will you have the year's first dance with me?"

Isabella kissed his cheek. "It's a deal."

Swaying in Nate's arms to the band's rendition of "I'll Be Home For Christmas," Isabella gazed at the lovely scene.

Beth, Owen, and the twins formed a circle holding hands and dancing together.

Kate, Anna, and newlywed Jen, dancing in the arms of their husbands.

The ring bearers chased each other in and out of the tables.

Sal sat next to Angie, and the two gazed into each other's eyes.

Charlie stood at the cookie table once again, devouring yet another of Dottie's cannoli cookies.

Isabella sensed her parents watching over her. *You both will always be here for me.* She melted into Nate's embrace. The locket pressed against her heart, and she remembered its inscription. "May all your once upon a times…end happily ever after."

The twinkling lights lining the tent's ceiling reminded Isabella of a starry night and the inspiring words on the poster in her childhood bedroom. She shot for the moon, and she hadn't missed. *I have landed exactly where I need to be, happily ever after.*

Christmas Cannoli Cookies

Cakey cookies with whole-milk ricotta and orange flavored glaze. Recipe makes 2 dozen cookies.

Cookie Ingredients:
Two cups all-purpose flour
One-half teaspoon baking soda
One-half teaspoon salt
One-half cup unsalted butter, softened at room temperature
One-fourths cup whole-milk ricotta, at room temperature
1 cup granulated sugar
One-half teaspoon orange zest
One-half teaspoon vanilla extract
One-half teaspoon almond extract
One-half teaspoon cinnamon
1 large egg, at room temperature
Three-fourths cup chocolate chips
Optional: shelled, halved pistachio nuts

Glaze Ingredients:
One-and-one-fourth sifted confectioners' sugar
One-half freshly squeezed seedless orange, or to taste
One-half teaspoon orange zest
One-half teaspoon almond extract
Optional: melted chocolate chips

Glaze Preparation:
Mix the ingredients with a whisk until thoroughly combined.

Cookie Preparation:

Heat oven to 350 degrees.

Using parchment paper, line baking sheets.

In a bowl, whisk flour with baking soda and salt until well-blended.

In a separate bowl, beat butter and ricotta about two minutes until fluffy (use hand mixer or a stand mixer with paddle attachment).

Add in sugar, orange zest, vanilla extract, almond extract, and cinnamon and beat about three minutes until blended.

Add the egg and beat until blended.

Blend in the flour mixture on low speed until blended.

Blend in the chocolate chips (and blend in nuts, optional).

Scrape the bowl, cover with plastic, refrigerate thirty minutes (or until firmer).

Drop batter about two inches apart by rounded tablespoon on the baking sheets.

Bake twelve minutes, until cookies are golden brown.

Cool for five minutes before glazing.

Glaze by dribbling or apply with pastry brush, your preference.

Optional: dip one side of glazed cookie into melted chocolate for half-and-half topping.

A word about the author…

Anne Armistead is an award-winning author of love stories, past and present. She earned her English literature degree from the University of Georgia and her MFA in Creative Writing from Spalding University. Anne is a member of the Atlanta Writers Club and the Historical Novel Society. She draws on her past career as an English teacher to present writing workshops and offers manuscript coaching services. Her historical romances include DANGEROUS CONJURINGS and WITH KISSES FROM CÉCILE, the winner of the 2020 Georgia Independent Author Award in historical fiction.
http://www.annearmisteadauthor.com

Thank you for purchasing
this publication of The Wild Rose Press, Inc.
For questions or more information
contact us at
info@thewildrosepress.com.
The Wild Rose Press, Inc.
www.thewildrosepress.com

Milton Keynes UK
Ingram Content Group UK Ltd.
UKHW020641050124
435493UK00011B/1407